Savage
Billionaire

Surprise Baby
Romance

Rebecca Baker

Sign up for my newsletter and receive a free romance novel:
https://BookHip.com/LHLBBPG

Chapter 1

Bridget

I tucked a strand of my auburn hair behind my ear as I listened intently to the order being rattled off to me from the perky blonde bride-to-be. She talked animatedly over the bar as I memorized her order. I never used a pen and paper anymore. This surprised people sometimes, but I had been doing this for years.

I watched as she walked back to her group of girlfriends in her white feather and sequin dress. I wondered what brought her here for her bachelorette party. There were plenty of clubs in the city, which was what they looked to be dressed for. Murphy's wasn't exactly a hot spot for bachelorette parties. It was more for sports-loving enthusiasts, especially Boston's beloved baseball fans who came for the big screen TVs, cheap beers, and frequent player sightings.

Ding. Ding. Ding. The bride's entourage was probably there to scope out the professional ballers. Murphy's had become their favorite place to come after games, since my father opened the place years ago. There were photos of the teams through the years all sitting in the bar or the coaches with their arms around my father's shoulders. He was a legend here in Boston.

When I was a young girl, I would come and sit at the bar doing homework while I sipped on Shirley Temples or watch the games on the weekend with the regulars. Sure, some would say it wasn't an appropriate place for someone my age, but I loved it. I loved being with my dad and he loved having me around. This place was his pride and joy, besides his family.

Some of the happiest times I had seen him were behind this very bar. Always a daddy's girl, I had made the decision when I was young that my dream would be to one day run this place. While it was pretty much a given, he would hand the place over to me when the time came, but I didn't want it to be that easy. I wanted to feel like I earned it, which was why, when I was old enough, I worked my ass off waitressing at a diner during the day and bartending here at night to earn enough to buy a share in the place. He never asked that of me, but he was proud.

When my dad fell ill a few years ago, I took over for him so he could focus on his health. Despite the circumstances, I was happy to be given the shot of running the place. I kept everything the same. Dim lighting, cheap drinks, greasy, but good food. There was no reason for changing something that worked. There was no reason to change a place that I loved.

I finished making a tray of house margaritas and walked it over to the bachelorette party. The women squealed in delight and clapped their hands at the sight of me. I let out a laugh as I set the tray down. They said thank you and then swooped in like vultures for their salt and lime. "Anything else I can get you ladies?" I asked, sliding the tray under my arm.

"Shots!" one bachelorette yelled, pumping her fists in the air.

"You've got it. Six tequila shots coming right up."

I turned to head back to the bar when one of the bachelorettes gently grabbed my arm and leaned in.

"Any chance any of the players will show up tonight?" She smiled mischievously at me.

"You never know at Murphy's." I winked.

The table of women giggled and looked around. The game had ended an hour ago, so there was a good chance the team would be heading here.

As I walked away, I heard one of them whisper, "I bet she's hooked up with one of them."

I shook my head slightly. They *were* a good-looking group of guys and wealthy beyond belief, but I had never had any romantic interest in any of them. Of course, I was friendly. Okay, maybe flirty, but that was just business. The players were a fun bunch, but none of them had ever crossed a line. Well, except for one and it wasn't with me, but with my former bartender. I banned him from the bar and he got kicked off the team for his behavior, so he got what was coming to him in the end.

I set my tray down at the bar and loaded it up with shot glasses. As I went to reach for a top shelf tequila, the bar top cleared and that was when I spotted her: Cara. My sister. What was she doing here? Whatever the reason for her turning up, it couldn't be good. As much as I loved my baby sister, trouble always followed. Things were going really good for me right now, and I didn't need anything mucking that up.

While I poured the shots, I snuck a few glances her way. I wondered how long she had been sitting there and why she hadn't said anything to me yet. I hadn't seen her or talked to her in months. You'd think she would at least say hello. The last I heard, she was in Ireland doing who knew what. I couldn't keep up with her, and despite pretending I didn't want to, the truth was I worried about her constantly.

I tried my best to put her out of my head and focus on the work at hand, but just knowing she was there felt like a black cloud was hovering above. I would have to deal with her at some point tonight. She *would* choose one of the busiest weekend nights to come ask for whatever help she needed from her big sister.

I balanced the tray on one hand as I walked over to the booth of the bachelorette party.

"Here are those shots, ladies. On the house."

They squealed in delight again. A few of them even stood and gave me sloppy hugs, which I accepted with a laugh. They clinked their glasses together and swallowed down the tequila, eagerly grabbing the lime wedges I had sliced for them. Just then, the door opened and I saw half the major league team walk in. Things were about to get really busy in here. Cara would have to wait.

"Oh, my God!" one of the bachelorettes said in a loud whisper as she looked toward the door.

"They're here," the bride said under her breath. "Play it cool."

"It's Kenny!" another one of them whispered.

"He's taken. Remember?"

"Why can't I be the cute baker girl he fell in love with?" one sighed.

"I'll leave you ladies to it." I tapped my knuckles on the table as I smiled to myself. Cleo had once worked here at the bar and was my good friend. I was happy she had found love and was now running a successful bakery not too far from here. The women continued gaping at the group of handsome men who were crowding up my entryway. I gently pushed my way through the crowded bar and greeted the team.

"That was one hell of a game, boys," I said, interrupting their chatter.

"Bridget!" they said in unison.

"Right this way."

I led them to their usual booth in the corner of the bar, where they plopped down with sighs of relief. I didn't blame them. After being tied at the ninth inning, they had gone on to play three more. It was a nail-biter of a game, and I had served many pints of beer to the viewers who had holed up here for hours. They ended up losing in the eleventh inning, bringing their season to a close much to everyone's dismay.

"What can I get you boys?" I asked as I leaned against the table. Despite losing, they seemed in good spirits.

"Whiskey to start," said one of the older players, Chad.

I knew he had a little crush on me because the team made it very obvious, much to his embarrassment. He was handsome, but not really my type. I still played along though. I didn't want to bruise anyone's ego.

"You've got it. Hey, that was a hell of a double play in the ninth," I commented, giving him a nod.

The rest of the table gave a loud "Ooooooooh," and Chad's face turned bright red.

He harrumphed. "It wasn't enough though."

"Hey now, you'll get them next season," I said assuredly.

I pushed off from the table and started toward the bar before turning around, "By the way, there's a group of bachelorettes over there who I know would be interested in talking to you boys." I nodded toward the other end of the bar.

Laughing, I watched the group of men literally levitate from their seats and strain their necks trying to get a good view. They deserved some fun tonight. As I made my way through the crowd, I looked toward the bar for Cara. I had better see what she wanted before this nagging feeling ruined my night. As I approached, I saw she wasn't alone.

I stood back and observed. He was an older man with broad shoulders in a navy suit. His hair was slicked back like he had spread grease through it. He talked intently with his hands and I noticed a fancy gold watch on his wrist, peeking through from the sleeve of his pressed shirt. There was no way this was a date, but then again, I never knew with my sister.

I watched as she sat across from him. She looked like a little girl being scolded as she cowered into herself. I should go over there and see what this was about. Whatever it was, it couldn't be good. I took a few swift steps toward them, but she spotted me and gave a discreet shake of the head. I stopped in my tracks. Whoever this guy was, she didn't want me interrupting. I wondered why.

Despite my better judgment, I granted her wish and stayed away. I ducked under the bar and continued working while stealing glances her way. Closer now, I could see the man looked angry. My sister was trying her best to calm him down. He caught me looking because he locked eyes with me before waving me over. I sucked in a breath. What mess was I being brought into?

"Can I help you?" I asked, but not before noticing Cara turn her back to me. Why was she pretending she didn't know me?

"I'll take a whiskey sour," the man said gruffly.

"Sure. Can I get you anything else?" I asked, looking at my sister.

"Nice place you got here," he said, looking around. He looked like an eagle stalking his prey, taking in every little detail of the bar. It was strange.

"Um, thank you. I'm very proud of it. I'll go make your drink."

After a few minutes, I walked back over and slid his drink across the bar top to him. I noticed my sister was gone. I looked around, trying to find her, but had no luck. The man in the suit slid me a twenty. I had hoped he would pay with a card, so I could at least get his name.

"Keep the change." He waved me off.

For the next twenty minutes I was busy entertaining the team, keeping the bachelorette party from getting thirsty, and helping my new bartender with whatever he needed. All the while trying to work out whatever was going on with my sister and this suspicious character she brought to the bar tonight.

Suddenly, I spotted her. She hadn't left after all. She was walking with the man to the exit. When he walked out the door, she turned and gave a meek wave before leaving after him. *That's it?* I hadn't seen her or heard from her in months and she showed up here to ignore me besides a small hand gesture? I felt heat creep up my neck to my cheeks. I was pissed, but I was also worried. The usual cocktail of emotions when it came to my sister. I would get to the bottom of this, but not tonight.

Chapter 2

Justin

I finished my mid-day cup of coffee and placed it in the sink as the doorbell rang. I glanced at my watch. 4 p.m. Right on time, which was surprising for Kenny. My best friend wasn't always punctual. I strode to the door and opened it to find him and his girlfriend standing in the doorway.

"Hey, Justin," he said.

"Hey, man. Hey, Cleo. Nice to see you." I pushed the door wide enough for them to enter. I patted Kenny on the back as he entered and gave Cleo a hug. I wasn't expecting her to join today, but I didn't mind at all. She was a good girl. The two of them were practically attached at the hip. I was happy for Kenny.

We made our way to the large charcoal gray sofa that sat in the center of the living room. The view of the city was crystal clear today as I looked out the windows that surrounded us. Kenny took a seat on the couch and pulled Cleo onto his lap. I couldn't help but roll my eyes.

"What?" asked Kenny, catching me.

"You two are like cats in heat."

Kenny laughed and Cleo blushed.

"What can I get you two? Water? Iced tea?"

"Water would be great," answered Cleo.

I walked to the kitchen and pulled down two glasses from the shelf, filling them with ice and water. When I got back to the living room, they had unattached themselves and looked like they were ready for business, which was why they were here. I was Kenny's financial assistant. Frequently, we would meet to go over his investments, stocks, and partnerships. He was the third baseman for the city's major league team. There were always a lot of moving parts.

"How are you feeling after last night?" I asked Kenny as I handed them their waters. The team had lost in the playoffs, but they had fought hard.

"Ahh. It is what it is. It just wasn't in the cards for us this season." Kenny took a sip of water.

"You played good, baby." Cleo patted his leg.

"And how is the bakery, Cleo?" She had just opened a bakery a few months ago, and it was already a morning hot spot in the city. It wasn't surprising because she was an amazing baker. I'd tried pastries from all the top cities in the world, and she was up there with some of the best patisseries.

"It's good. Busy. Really busy, but I love it." She beamed.

"She finally got someone she trusted to run the shop, which is why she's here with me. Time is rare with the city's top baker," said Kenny.

She nudged him with her shoulder and rolled her eyes.

"Well, should we get down to it?" I asked, opening the small stack of folders that rested on the coffee table.

For the next hour we went over all of Kenny's assets, went over stock stats, and discussed potential endorsements from a few athletic lines. The guy had it made, but it wasn't like he didn't work his ass off for all he had.

"Well, that's it for today. I'll look over the budgets for each endorsement and let you know which one seems most solid." I closed the folder and tossed it on the coffee table.

"Thanks, man. Are you up for lunch?" Kenny asked as he stretched his arms above his head.

"Yeah, sure. Are you sure you want me to tag along on your date though?"

"You're always welcome, Justin," said Cleo warmly.

"Any suggestions?" asked Kenny.

"Actually, I was thinking we could pop into Murphy's. I haven't seen any of my old coworkers in a little while. Is that okay?" asked Cleo.

"Sure. I could go for a beer. What do you say, Justin?" asked Kenny. The Irish pub wasn't a place I frequented much, but the few times I had gone it was a fun time.

"I'll drive." I stood from the couch and walked to the entryway table, grabbing my keys.

Murphy's wasn't far from my place. It was about a five-minute drive, most of which Kenny and Cleo made out in the backseat. I couldn't help but feeling like a chaperone to a middle school dance. I laughed to myself in the front seat and turned the classic rock radio station up. Soon, we pulled up to the bar. I found an open meter and parked on the curb.

When we walked inside, it took a moment for my eyes to adjust to the dim lighting. There were a few old men holed up at the bar. Regulars, I assumed. The rest of the place was pretty dead. I knew it would pick up later. The times I had been here it had been out celebrating with Kenny and the team. The place was always packed.

We found a corner booth and took a seat. A bartender approached with menus.

"You must be my replacement!" said Cleo with an enthusiastic wave.

"Are you the famous Cleo?" asked the bartender.

"That's me." She held out her hand.

"I'm Andy." He shook her hand.

"This is my fiancé, Kenny. And this is Justin."

"Nice to meet you guys. What can I get you to drink?"

"Can we get a round of draft beer?" I asked.

"On it."

We all studied the menu for a millisecond. There wasn't much on it, but the fish and chips sounded good. When the beers came, we ordered our food and began talking about the following baseball season. Kenny was locked into a four-year contract, but I was curious about a few other players.

While he rattled on about some of the newbies, I couldn't help but notice the woman behind the bar. I had seen her a few times before, but had never actually met her. She was stunning. How had I not noticed it before? Maybe the bar had always been too crowded and busy, but even then, I was sure she would stick out.

I tried to focus on what Kenny was saying, but my eyes kept moving to her. She stood behind the bar with her red hair pulled effortlessly into a clip, except for a few unruly pieces that hung by her face. She was on the phone and I wondered who she was talking to. It didn't seem like it was a good conversation based on her furrowed brow and low voice. She sounded angry, but what really stood out to me was her accent. It was a mix of the city, but a little bit of Irish, too. It melted like butter, even when she was upset.

Cleo must have followed my gaze because she looked worried all of a sudden.

"I'll be right back." She slid from the booth and walked toward the bar.

"What's her name again?" I nodded toward the bartender.

Kenny followed my nod. "Bridget. She owns the place. You've met her, haven't you?"

"Not officially."

"Would you like to?" Kenny wiggled his eyebrows at me.

"Looks like she's in the middle of something."

Cleo was waiting patiently at the bar for her friend to finish her phone call. With a frustrated sigh, Bridget hung up the phone. It seemed abrupt. I wondered if she had hung up on whoever was on the other line. Her frustration was short-lived when she saw Cleo. She ducked under the bar door and wrapped her arms around Cleo. They did a little dance while they hugged. They talked animatedly and quickly. I couldn't make out what they were saying.

Cleo glanced over to our booth and I looked away quickly to not be caught staring.

"She's on her way over." Kenny nudged me.

"Shut up." I muttered under my breath.

"Kenny! It's good to see you," Bridget said warmly.

Kenny stood and gave her a hug. "It's good to see you too, Bridget. Have you met my friend, Justin?"

I looked up and met her eyes. They were a deep green and they were staring right at me. Her skin was ivory and there was a sprinkle of small freckles across the bridge of her nose. She looked even better up close.

"Hello. It's nice to meet you," I said, holding out my hand.

She took it and shook it gently. She studied me for a second and raised one of her eyebrows. "I've seen you here before, haven't I?"

"Yeah, I've been in a few times when I was visiting from New York."

"But he lives here now," Kenny interjected.

"Well, welcome to Boston," she said. Her smile was infectious. I would have gotten lost in it if it weren't for my phone ringing. I slid it out of my pocket and saw my dad on the caller ID. My good mood immediately left. I squeezed out of the booth.

"Sorry, you'll have to excuse me." I walked to the door and stepped outside.

"Hi, Dad," I answered.

"What's this I hear about you working remote? What happened to obtaining an office space?" he asked. No greeting. Straight into it.

"It makes more sense to work remote while I build a clientele in the city. Everyone is working from home these days."

"You're not everyone. How are you going to establish yourself without an office? Maybe Boston was a bad idea. You left a cush high-rise in New York to what... work in your pajamas?"

"That's not what I'm doing, Dad."

"You're better than that."

I took a deep breath and bit my tongue. My dad was old-fashioned in many ways, but especially when it came to business. He didn't understand that times were changing. Jobs looked a lot different these days. It didn't matter that I had retained my clientele from New York, and had since been building a solid clientele in Boston based on referrals. It didn't matter how many times I tried to explain it or prove myself, it wasn't enough.

"And when are you coming home?"

I rolled my eyes. What son would want to come home to *that?*

"Your mother misses you."

"I know that. I promise I'll be out soon," I lied.

I heard him harrumph on the other line before he said he had to go and hung up. I leaned against the bar and closed my eyes for a minute. It was always the same thing with him. I was a disappointment. I wasn't measuring up. Just once, it would be nice if he could say he was proud of me. At least he was doing me one favor. He was showing me exactly how not to be as a father.

I didn't know if I wanted kids. I'd probably need to find a wife first. I was getting ahead of myself. I'd need to find a girlfriend before that. If we did decide to raise a family, I wanted to be nothing like my father. Sure, people could say his tough love was what made me into the businessman I was. I wondered often if it was worth it.

I looked at my phone and sighed. I knew I shouldn't have answered. He had ruined my mood. I didn't want to go back in the bar and ruin everyone else's evening or look like an ass to the cute owner. Instead, I texted Kenny:

Hey, man. Something came up. Dinner's on me next time. Call an Uber on me.

Kenny: *Is everything okay?*

Me: *Yeah. All good. Talk to you later.*

I climbed into my car and began the drive home. The clear skies from earlier seemed like a dark cloud had covered them. It was probably just me, though.

Chapter 3

Bridget

It was nice to see Cleo again, even though she came in during my heated conversation with Cara. I missed her working with me. Plus, the cute guy she introduced me to helped my bad mood a little. I knew I had seen him in here before with the team, but he was quieter than the rest of the team, who were always puffing their chests out and trying to be the loudest people in the room. Justin? Was that his name? Whoever he was, I didn't get a chance to talk to him much today because he left suddenly.

It was a slow afternoon, so I was able to sit and catch up with Cleo and Kenny. I still can't believe she landed her bakery and the love of her life all at the same time. She deserved it. I was happy for her. They were like puppies in love—and in heat. They didn't have any issues with PDA, which made me laugh. It also made me feel a little lonely. Between running the bar, caring for my dad, and constantly worrying about my sister, there wasn't a lot of time for love. Most of the time it didn't bother me, but when it was smack-dab in my face, a little loneliness crept in.

When they left, I gave Cleo a big hug and we said our goodbyes. I promised to stop by her bakery soon. Once they left there was a lull, which left me alone with my thoughts. My messy thoughts. I sat in a corner booth and leaned my head back, letting out a sigh. Cara. Wherever she goes, trouble follows.

After she had come into the bar last night with that greasy-looking older gentleman, I decided to call her today and see what was up. I thought it was going to go to voicemail, which wouldn't be surprising, but then she picked up. It sounded like she had just woken up. It was nearly 6 p.m.

I replayed the conversation in my head.

"Hello?" she said, her voice sounding muffled.

"Cara?"

"Who is this?"

"Uh, your sister. Bridget. Remember me? Or do you pretend you don't know me nowadays?"

"Oh, sorry, sis. I'm just swamped in work."

"Really? Because it sounds like you are half asleep." I rolled my eyes.

"Are you calling to judge me as usual?"

"No, I'm calling to see why you were in my bar last night. I haven't heard from you in months and then you just show up here and completely ignore me."

She remained silent on the other line. I wondered if she had fallen asleep.

"Cara!" I said loudly.

"I'm here," she replied quietly.

"Out with it."

Another pause. I waited impatiently. Whatever it was, I knew it wasn't good.

"I came to see you. I missed you."

"Mhmm," I said, unconvinced.

"I did have something to talk with you about, but I got wrapped up with a, um, business partner."

"What do you need, Cara?" I asked, closing my eyes and holding the bridge of my nose with my fingers.

"Well, a business opportunity came up."

"Oh, like the food truck you were going to open? Or the clothing boutique? Or the pyramid scheme?"

"What happened to not judging?"

"Okay, sorry. I'm listening."

"I just need a little bit of money to get it up and running."

I closed my eyes. "What's a little?"

Another pause.

"Ten grand."

I slammed my hand on the table. "Ten grand?" I shouted.

She hesitated again. "I know it seems like a lot, but I'll pay it back."

"You think I just have ten grand lying around?" I groaned.

"The bar is successful. I saw for myself last night."

"And it costs a lot to run this place. I don't have that kind of money," I snapped.

I thought how even if I did, I sure as hell would not give it to Cara. She practically bled money. Apparently, she thought it grew on trees, or in my yard. I couldn't believe what I was hearing. I didn't even know what the business venture was. I didn't even *want* to know. It was just going to be another failure, and I wanted nothing to do with it. She better not have gone to Dad asking for money, either. He was in no shape to be dealing with her messy life.

"Fine. I don't need you. I'll figure this out on my own. Like I always do."

Lies. I couldn't count the number of times I had helped her get out of a jam. I was about to remind her of this, but that was when I spotted Cleo at a table.

"You better not drag Dad into whatever mess you're in or whatever mess you're about to be in. Next time you come to my bar, it better be because you miss me, and not because you need something." I hung up on her.

I let the conversation brew in my head for a little while longer, until my thoughts were interrupted by a few regulars coming in to watch the playoffs, even though their team hadn't made it. I welcomed the distraction. The rest of the night, I was on autopilot.

When I got home at 4 a.m., I took a quick shower and climbed into bed. I was exhausted, but sleep didn't come easy. I kept thinking about Cara and what preposterous reason she needed all that money for. As much as she stressed me out, I still loved her. She was my sister. I still had so many questions for her. Like, who was the guy in the suit? Why did she ignore me? I knew I had to let it go. She was old enough to figure it out. I finally fell asleep at 7 a.m.

At around 11, I rolled out of bed and threw on some sweats. I decided to go visit Cleo at her bakery. A hot cup of coffee and a blueberry muffin sounded good. A nice walk in the city would do me good.

When I walked through the door of the bakery, I was hit with the smell of fresh cinnamon rolls and dark roast coffee. The place was packed. Cleo was behind the counter, taking orders while filling the display case. She looked busy, but happy. I knew the feeling. Murphy's was my dream. This was hers. The days were long, but always worth it.

When she spotted me, she waved me over and gave me a hug over the counter. "You came!"

"I said I would. I needed one of your blueberry muffins, and coffee."

"Coming right up!" She grabbed a plate and the biggest muffin from the glass case. She poured a cup of coffee in a pale blue *Cleo's* mug.

"Hey, Annie! Can you watch the front? I'm going to take a break," she called out.

"Sure thing, boss!" a voice called out from the kitchen.

"Let's sit! Come!" Cleo grabbed my coffee and muffin and led me to a quiet table that was tucked in the back.

I took a sip of coffee and took a deep breath as it ran through my body. This was just what I needed.

"Long night?" Cleo asked, raising her eyebrows in concern.

"Always. Especially when Cara is around."

Her eyes widened. "She's in town again?"

"Apparently. She came in the bar Friday night."

"Wow. What's new with her?" she inquired.

"Other than needing ten grand, nothing."

"What?" Cleo spat out.

"Yeah, that's who I was on the phone with yesterday when you came in."

"I'm sorry, Bridg."

"It's okay. I should be used to it by now. Let's change the subject. Who was that guy you brought in yesterday?"

"Justin? You thought he was cute, huh?" She did a little dance in her seat.

"Okay, calm down." I shook my head as I took a bite of my blueberry muffin.

"He's Kenny's best friend. Super nice. Super successful."

"Super hot," I added, smiling into my cup.

"I *knew* you thought he was cute. I saw that smile you gave him."

I rolled my eyes. "I doubt he's interested in a bar owner."

"What? Why?"

"He seems high class."

She gave me a casual wave. "Hardly. He's actually really down to earth."

"What does he do?" I asked.

"He's a financial advisor."

"Oh, perfect. Maybe he can help Cara out," I muttered sarcastically.

Cleo gave me a look before reaching over and giving my hand a squeeze. "Don't let her get to you, okay?"

I nodded, but that was all I did for the rest of the weekend. Let her get to me. I tried calling her again. Twice, but she didn't answer. I called my dad, mostly to check on him, but to also see if he would mention anything. He didn't, and I didn't want to bring Cara up. He worried too much about her.

When Monday rolled around, I drove to work and saw a town car parked right outside the entrance in an unmetered spot. I peered inside as I pulled my car into the back alley and could have sworn I saw the same guy who was with Cara a few nights before. When I parked, I walked to the front, but he was already pulling away. I couldn't get a good look at him, but I swore it was him. Suddenly, I had a bad feeling in my stomach.

I walked inside the bar feeling stressed. My staff could tell. They were on edge during our afternoon meeting, watching me carefully. I was in no mood to work, which was rare for me. I loved the bar. It was my second home. It was on the rare nights like these that I wished I had my dad to run the place, or another partner. But I didn't. I had to suck it up and put a smile on. The last thing I needed was to take out my bad mood on any customers.

Thankfully, there was no game tonight and it was a weekday. It would most likely be a slow night. One that I could fill with liquor inventory and organizing the shipment. Tasks that I would normally delegate to my staff, but tonight I welcomed them because I wanted to keep my mind busy.

At 10 p.m., the bar suddenly erupted into cheers. I looked up curiously and to my surprise, the team was walking through the front door. What were they doing here on a Monday night? This was not their usual night. It wasn't even their season anymore. What win was there to celebrate or what loss was there to drown out? I suddenly felt irritated.

They stood by the door, talking loudly amongst themselves and waiting to be seated. I was usually the one to greet them, flirt with them, boost their egos, take them to their usual corner booth. I had no desire to play hostess tonight. I stayed behind the bar watching them look around for me like lost puppies.

"Andy!" I called out.

"Yeah, boss?" He was drying glasses and putting them on the shelves.

"Can you take care of the team tonight?" I nodded toward the players.

"Really?" he asked, raising his eyebrows in surprise. He was no Cleo, but he would have to do. Sure, he was new, but he'd be a better host than me tonight. I didn't want to make a bad impression on our biggest customers. Part of the appeal of Murphy's was brushing shoulders with some of the best players in the league. If that went away, so would a lot of my business.

"Go," I said, waving him away. I took over drying the glasses for him.

I could see from the corner of my eye some of the players looking confused when they saw Andy walking up with menus. Chad was looking around for me disappointedly. They'd get over it. I just needed to keep my head down and work. I'd leave the schmoozing and socializing to the other staff. Just for tonight. I'd be in a better mood tomorrow. When dealing with Cara, there was always a three-day hangover before the cloud lifted and I felt myself again.

Chapter 4

Justin

I sat on the couch flipping through channels and settled for an action movie I had seen before. I had wrapped up all my meetings earlier in the day, and now I was bored. I guessed one thing I missed about being in an office was there were usually coworkers to go grab happy hour with.

My phone buzzed on the coffee table. I picked it up and saw a text from Kenny:

Hey. Cleo's closing today. Want to grab a late lunch?

Me: *Wow. You're so whipped.*

Kenny: *Shut up. You want to or not?*

Me: *I'm game.*

Kenny: *Cool. I'll be there in ten.*

Ten minutes later, I pushed through the glass doors of my building as I saw Kenny pull up in his black sports car. He annoyingly honked three times, as he always did, making me rush to get in the car before he pissed off my neighbors. I climbed in the passenger seat and he grinned at me.

"You're pleased with yourself, aren't you?" I asked, closing the door and putting on my seatbelt.

"I like watching you sweat." He put the car into drive and peeled out of the entrance to my condo.

"So, where are we grabbing lunch?"

"I was thinking Murphy's."

"Again?"

"I like it there. Plus, you didn't really get a chance to try the food." He shrugged.

I gave a single nod. I wished I had known, so I could have maybe put on something other than a wrinkled shirt and sweats. I wanted to see that cute bartender again, but not like this. Oh, well. There was no changing now. I looked out the window and watched as the city whizzed past us. Boston was growing on me. New York was great, but I liked the people in Boston better. It helped that my best friend was here too.

"Sooo…" Kenny said slyly.

"What?"

"I hear Bridget thinks you're hot," he replied, watching the road as he weaved in and out of cars.

"What? Really?" That got my attention.

Kenny laughed.

"That's cool. Whatever," I said, trying to play it off like it was nothing.

"Maybe try talking to her today, instead of rushing off to who knows where."

"Yeah. Sorry about that. It was my dad."

"You can't let him get to you, man." Kenny shook his head. He knew all about the complicated relationship I had with my father. His own was complicated, too. Way more complicated than mine. Still, it was nice to have someone who understood.

Soon, we were pulling in front of Murphy's. Kenny parked in a metered spot in front of the bar entrance. While Kenny put change in the meter, I smoothed my hair quickly, trying to be inconspicuous, but Kenny saw and laughed to himself.

We pushed through the bar doors and found a high-top near the back to sit at. The same guy who took our order last time approached.

"Good to see you guys again. No Cleo today?" he asked, as he handed us menus.

"She's working at the bakery," said Kenny.

"I still need to make it over there. Bridget says it's incredible."

"It is. I'm very proud."

I watched as Kenny beamed over his fiancée. This was a whole different guy than the one I knew. He used to be jaded from a pretty bad breakup, but Cleo had changed him for the better. Even though I was still living the bachelor life, if you could even call it that, I was glad we still had time for a pint.

"What can I get you guys?" asked Andy, tapping his pen on his paper pad.

"We will start with two pints, please," I said.

"On it."

I looked around the bar briefly to see if Bridget was there, but I didn't spot her behind the bar. I furrowed my brows slightly.

"She's probably in the back," said Kenny.

"Who?" I asked, acting clueless.

Kenny shook his head. Andy brought over frosted mugs of beer and slid them across the table. We clinked our glasses together and got down to business.

"So, this deal with the athleticwear line, what do you think?" asked Kenny, looking at me expectantly.

I slid my phone from my pocket and opened my emails. I glanced over the contract Kenny had forwarded me once again. I had already studied it when he initially sent it.

"Based on the contract, I think it's a good one. You'd be locked in for two years and there is the obvious non-compete clause. You'd have to live and breathe it."

"I already do, so that's not a problem."

"I think you should do it then. I'll have my lawyer look it over to make sure everything is kosher. If it is, you'll be six million dollars richer."

Kenny did a little fist bump.

"Okay, what do you think about the supplement line?" he asked.

I really should have brought my laptop, I thought. This was turning into a full-fledged business meeting. It would be good to have all the figures and contracts in front of me, rather than scrolling on my phone. We made do though, and continued talking business until we finished our beers.

"Do you boys need another round?" a woman's voice said. Smooth as butter with a hint of Irish.

I looked up quickly. Too quickly. There she was. Red hair falling past her shoulders in soft waves, lips pressed into a warm smile, and those deep green eyes.

"Um, what do you think, Kenny?" I cleared my throat.

"Two more, please, Bridget. Can we put in an order for two fish and chips too?"

"You've got it. Are you actually going to stay and eat the food this time?" She looked at me and raised a brow.

"Yeah. I'm not going anywhere," I answered.

She smiled and walked back toward the bar.

"I'm not going anywhere?" Kenny mocked me.

"Shut up. Now about this other contract." I looked intently at my phone.

"Incoming. Five o'clock," said Kenny under his breath.

I looked up and saw two women whispering to each other as they approached the table. One was a petite brunette wearing a red tank top dress. The other was a taller blonde wearing cutoff jean shorts and a black T-shirt. Her legs were killer. I sat up and leaned back against the barstool, stretching my hands behind my head.

"Signature Justin move," Kenny whispered as he rolled his eyes.

I shot him a look before smiling at the approaching women.

"Sorry to interrupt," said the brunette.

"Please do," I said.

"Are you Kenny Michaels?" she asked.

"I am. And you are?" asked Kenny casually.

"I'm Carly," said the brunette. She was practically oozing over Kenny.

"And I'm Aly," said the blonde, looking at me.

"And I'm Justin," I said.

We shook their hands and they leaned against the high-top. I suspected they wanted us to invite them to sit with us, but I knew Kenny wouldn't want that. He was an engaged man.

"Are you guys looking to party?" asked Carly, looking expectantly at Kenny.

"At three o'clock on a Wednesday?" asked Kenny.

They both giggled.

"Well, no. But later?"

"Sorry, ladies. I am spoken for by my fiancée."

Carly looked disappointed, but Aly looked at me and smiled mischievously.

"And what about you, Justin? Are you spoken for?"

"Nope."

"Good," she said, biting her lip slightly before reaching into her purse. She pulled out her phone and unlocked it.

"What's your Snapchat?" she asked.

I barely used Snapchat, but it did come in handy when I didn't want to give my number out. I gave her my handle and she typed it into her phone. Just then, Andy arrived at the table with our food.

"It was nice to meet you, ladies," said Kenny, unwrapping his silverware to eat.

They looked a little disappointed, knowing the conversation was over, but they gave a little wave as they walked away and went back to their table across the bar. As they sat down, I saw Aly snap a quick selfie and then my phone buzzed. She had sent me a snap. I smiled slightly before putting my phone in my pocket.

"That was here, wasn't it?" Kenny eyed me.

"What?" I shrugged, "She was cute."

"Are you going to snap her back? Who even snaps anymore?" he asked with a smirk.

"Oh, shut up. It wasn't too long ago when you were doing the same thing."

"Hey, I'm still a pretty good wingman!" said Kenny between bites of food.

"Hardly." I took my first bite of food. It was delicious. I looked at the fried fish and around the bar. It was better than I expected for a place like this.

"Good, right?" asked Kenny, taking a sip of beer.

"Very."

As we finished our beer and food, I snuck a few glances at the bar where Bridget was. She kept busy stocking the shelves and serving customers. She looked totally in her element. I could tell she loved what she did. I liked watching her.

Kenny and I both cleared our plates and pint glasses. I sat back and let out a deep breath. I was so full.

"How did you like it? Now that you actually stayed to try it?" asked Bridget as she sidled up to the table.

"Delicious. I think I found my new favorite spot in the city."

I wasn't lying either. I liked the dim lighting, the wood finishes, the come-as-you-are feeling. Most of my business meetings were at fancy, expensive restaurants, which were fine. I enjoyed myself, but it was nice to come somewhere that didn't have so much prestigiousness.

"I'm glad you enjoyed it. Let me take your plates." Bridget reached over and started stacking our empty plates and gathering our empty glasses. Her perfume smelled nice, like fresh linen.

"I'll be right back with the bill," she said as she walked away, balancing everything one-handed on a tray.

I let my eyes wander as her back was turned. She wore a pair of light denim jeans and a black shirt with *Murphy's* on the back. I wanted to talk to her more, but didn't want to in front of Kenny. He would never let me live it down.

"Um, I'll be right back," I said. My eyes never leaving her.

"Mhmm." Kenny leaned back in his chair and followed the direction my eyes were pointed. He was enjoying this way too much.

When I approached the bar, Bridget was punching in numbers on the cash register. I leaned against the counter and waited for her to finish. As the bill printed out, she looked up and saw me.

"Oh, hello," she said, looking at me questioningly.

"Hi. I thought I'd save you the trip."

"Thanks. My feet thank you for not making me walk those ten steps. Here is your bill." She ripped the paper from the printer.

"Thank you." I rummaged in my back pocket for my wallet. I handed her my card and watched her run it through the machine.

"So, when are you off?" I asked.

Bridget glanced at the clock. It was nearly 5 p.m.

"Eleven hours from now."

"Oh." I tried hiding my disappointment.

"Yeah. Don't you have plans already?" She nodded toward the two women from earlier who were eyeing me from their table. Had she been listening to our conversation? I fought back a smile at the thought she might be interested.

"I'm more into redheads," I said casually.

Bridget rolled her eyes as she handed me back my card. "I'll see you around," she said.

You can count on it, I thought.

Chapter 5

Bridget

I smiled to myself as the cute guy, Justin, walked out of the bar. He gave a little wave before he stepped out the door after Kenny. He had been so corny with that line about redheads, but I kind of liked it. He seemed nice enough. Plus, he was easy on the eyes.

When the door opened again, I half expected it to be him coming back in to get my number or something, but to my disappointment it was Cara. I had called her several times since she had been in here, but she never called back. She hadn't returned any of my texts. Now she was strolling in here and smiling at me like nothing was wrong.

I leaned against the back bar and crossed my arms as I let out a sigh.

"Good to see you, too, sis," she said, taking a seat on a barstool in front of me.

"Don't *sis* me."

I watched as she rolled her eyes, which just pissed me off more.

"What now?" she asked, exasperated.

"Oh, I don't know. You haven't called me back or texted me back. I've been worried about you."

She rolled her eyes. "You're not my mom."

Ugh. She was such a brat sometimes.

"Well, did you get everything figured out?"

"With what?" she asked, reaching over the bar and pouring herself a coke.

"The insane amount of money you were asking me for."

"Oh that. Yeah, I figured it out." She nodded

"Wait, you got the money?" I questioned, not believing what I was hearing.

"Yeah." She shrugged nonchalantly.

"Where the hell did you get ten grand from, Cara?"

"I have my ways." She took a sip of her drink.

I knew better than to push her. Sometimes I had to walk on eggshells to stay close to my sister to keep her safe. If I pushed or prodded too hard, she fled. That was why she had been in Ireland or wherever for months before coming back home.

"How long are you in town for?" I asked, changing the subject.

"We'll see. You know me. I'm never anywhere for too long."

"Have you seen Dad yet?" I asked.

"I stopped by this morning for breakfast. He looks like he's doing better."

"He is." *Thanks to me,* I couldn't help but thinking.

The truth was, it was a lot taking care of him and running this place. Without my mom around and my flaky sister, I was really the only one he could count on. I felt like I was running on empty most days, but lately his health did seem to be improving. I had been dropping off prepped meals, making trips to the pharmacy, and making sure he got outside for some fresh air. The past six months had been hard, but worth it to see him feeling better.

"Where are you staying?" She was evicted from her apartment last month after missing two months' worth of payments while she was out of the country. Clearly, she wasn't staying with our dad if she had "stopped by" this morning.

"A friend's," she said vaguely.

"Always with the secrets," I said, rolling my eyes.

"Life is more fun that way." She winked.

"Look, I—"

"I gotta go," she interrupted me. She finished her drink and set it on the counter.

"But—"

"Thanks for the refreshments. Love ya." She grabbed her purse and gave a little wave over her shoulder as she made her way to the door.

"Love you," I whispered.

The rest of the week dragged on. I didn't see Cara again. I also didn't see Justin again. I couldn't say I wasn't a little disappointed. I thought maybe there was something there, or at least the start of something. Who was I kidding, though? I didn't have time to date. Between the bar, my dad, and my elusive sister, there was no time.

Except for Sundays. Sundays the bar was closed. My dad had always said it was family day. I had very fond memories of our Sundays together, whether we were catching a ball game at the stadium or going to the park for a picnic or staying home to watch movies. It was always *our* day.

So, when Sunday rolled around, I looked forward to having the day away from the bar to do whatever I wanted. Usually, after visiting with my dad in the morning, I would spend most of the day vegging out on the couch. But today, I wanted to enjoy some sunshine.

In the morning, I spent a few hours cooking. I made a few different meals and packed them in glass containers. Then I drove over to the suburbs to my dad's house to drop off his food for the week. When I pulled into the driveway, he was sitting on the porch reading. He hadn't heard my car. I sat in the car for a minute just watching him. He looked happy, which made me smile.

"Hey, Dad," I said as I opened the car door and stepped out.

"Bridget. Right on time," he said with a little wave.

I opened the trunk and grabbed the stack of meals. I carefully walked up the steps of the porch, giving my dad a quick kiss on the cheek before making my way inside. It was my childhood home and everything looked pretty much the same. It was my safe place.

I made my way to the kitchen and set the meals on the counter before organizing the fridge. I stacked them in the order which he should cook them and had written out Post-It notes with cooking times and temperatures. It was probably overkill, but I worried. Too much, probably.

When I was finished, I met my dad on the porch. He gently closed his book and patted the chair next to him. My mom's chair. I took a seat and rocked slowly back and forth.

"How are you, Dad?"

"I'm good. Better than ever," he said with a reassuring smile.

"Good. Cara said she came by. Said you looked healthy."

He nodded. "That sister of yours is a real firecracker. Gets that from your mom."

"Don't I know it."

"And how are you, Bridg?" he asked, looking at me intently.

"I'm good, Dad." I patted his hand.

"You look tired."

"Gee, thanks," I replied sarcastically.

45

"You're doing too much. You do too much for me. I always say it. I'm okay, honey."

I shrugged. "I know."

"Don't worry so much about me." He gave my hand a squeeze.

"I'll try."

"You should spend less time here and more time trying to find someone who can give me grandkids."

"Dad!" I practically shouted.

"What? I'm not getting any younger. Lord knows your little sister isn't going to give me any, anytime soon."

"I should hope not!" I smirked.

We both laughed at that. We spent the next hour on the porch. I made us some grilled cheese and tomato soup, and we talked over lunch. We talked about the bar and baseball season. Two of his favorite things. When it was time for his nap, I walked him inside and hugged him goodbye.

Seeing him in good health put me in good spirits. I decided to not waste the day on the couch and headed to the park in the city where we would go as kids. I grabbed some lunch from my favorite sandwich shop and an extra piece of bread to feed the ducks. When I got to the park, I found an empty bench by the little lake and ate in the sunshine. When I finished eating, I tore pieces of bread and tossed them to the ducks. It was a beautiful day. I was surprised there weren't more people there.

I leaned my head against the back of the bench and closed my eyes for a few minutes. I heard someone clear their throat. I opened my eyes quickly and saw Justin standing there, looking at me curiously.

"Um, hi." I sat up straight. I was not expecting to see him. He looked like he had been out for a run. His gray shirt was slightly wet with sweat and I couldn't help notice how it clung to his upper arms. He pulled his headphones out from his ears.

"I thought that was you," he said. "I saw your red hair from across the lake."

I smiled as I tucked my hair behind my ears.

He eyed the seat next to me. "Can I ...?"

"Oh, yeah. Sure, sit." I patted the bench next to me.

He sat down and we both sat in silence for a minute. The silence wasn't uncomfortable, but I felt excited. Expectant. This was a pleasant surprise.

"So, do you come here often?" I asked, immediately regretting it because it sounded like a pickup line. He bit back a smile and my eyes disobediently wandered to his lips.

"There's a great running path. It's no Central Park, but I like it."

"Is that where you're from? New York?"

"Yeah. I moved here a few months ago. Kenny persuaded me."

"Wise move. Boston over New York any day."

"Is that so?" he asked with a grin.

I lifted my chin. "Yup."

"Well, I have to say the women have exceeded my expectations." He smiled at me.

I couldn't help but laugh. He was so corny, but also smooth at the same time. Was he like this with everyone? I wondered if he was naturally flirtatious. It was probably built into his DNA. He seemed like the type. I was witness to it at the bar with those two women the other day. It seemed like every hair color was his type, but I ignored those thoughts and decided to enjoy his company for a little while.

"Have you lived here all your life?" he asked, realizing his line had fallen flat.

"Born and raised," I said proudly.

We continued talking about anything and everything. I learned what I already knew, which was that he was a financial advisor. He didn't seem cocky talking about it. It seemed like he genuinely enjoyed his job and wasn't in it just for the money. I'd met enough bigwigs in the city to know who was in it for the right reasons.

He asked a lot of questions about the bar, which I happily talked about. He seemed interested in what I had to say. He was also pretty funny. I caught myself genuinely laughing a lot.

Like real belly laughs. Not the kind I faked at the bar for tips.

After some time, I checked the time. We had been talking for two hours. How could that be?

"Oh shoot," I said, looking at my phone.

"What is it?"

"I didn't realize how late it was," I said, gathering my things.

"Do you have somewhere you need to be?" he asked. I heard a little disappointment in his voice. I felt it too, which was why I didn't know why I was leaving so suddenly. Maybe it was because I hadn't actually gotten lost in a conversation with a man in a long time. Maybe it was because this could actually be something, and that scared me. So, I lied.

"Yeah, I actually have a date," I blurted out. I regretted it as soon as I said it.

"Oh," Justin said quietly.

"Yeah, sorry. I'll see you around." I slung my purse over my shoulder and began walking to my car.

On the drive home, I wondered why I had lied. He seemed perfectly nice. Easy to talk to. Successful. Hot. Ugh. I totally screwed that up. Oh, well. We could be acquaintances. Friends even. He was a close friend of Kenny's and the team's. I needed to stay on their good side. I had rocked the boat enough last year when I exiled one of their players, even though he deserved it. They had all backed me up on it.

It was probably better this way. Relationships could be messy, and the last thing I needed was more of a mess.

Chapter 6

Justin

I sat on the bench a little while longer, wondering why Bridget had left so abruptly. Maybe she did really have a date, or maybe she was just making an excuse to get the hell out of here. I thought we were hitting it off well. She seemed really down to earth. The truth was, I had lost track of time too. I didn't remember the last time that had happened during a conversation with a woman. It was a nice change.

I popped my headphones back in my ears and headed up the sidewalk toward the noise of the city. It was funny how a park like this could make you forget you were in a major city. I was happy I had found it while exploring a few weeks ago. I had been trying to get my bearings in Boston. As many times as I had come and visited, the only places I had really ever gone were to the clubs with the team or fancy restaurants with clients. I still had much to explore. So far, I had found a running path and an Irish pub.

On Monday morning, I headed to the grocery store down the block from my condo to do my shopping for the week. I pulled a cart from the lineup and began perusing the aisles. I actually enjoyed grocery shopping, but not as much as I loved cooking. That surprised some people, but I grew up cooking with my mom in the kitchen. Despite the groaning and grunting from my father about how men didn't belong in the kitchen, I loved that time with my mom.

I pulled my shopping list from my pocket and began reading what I needed. As I turned a corner, I accidentally rammed my cart into someone else's.

"I'm so sorry," I said, looking up to see who I had collided with.

To my surprise, it was Bridget. She was wearing leggings, an oversized band tee, and high-tops. Her hair was pulled up into a messy bun. She looked casually cool. Her eyes widened when she saw me.

"Are you stalking me? Should I be worried?" she asked as she pretended to look around for help.

"I told you I had a thing for redheads." I laughed. "But no, not stalking. Just looking for the condiment aisle."

"Aisle four." She pointed to the left.

"Thanks."

I noticed she had a lot of food in her cart. I wasn't one to judge, but I was curious if she had a roommate or a boyfriend. It seemed like a lot for just her. She must have noticed me eyeing everything in her cart.

"See anything you like?" she asked, raising an eyebrow.

"Uh, no. Sorry. It's just a lot of food for one person—"

"Wow. Judging a girl for how much she eats." She crossed her arms.

"Er, no. I would never. I just…" I could feel myself start to sweat.

"I'm messing with you."

I breathed a sigh of relief.

"I help my dad out with groceries. I shop and meal prep for him."

"Oh. That's really nice of you."

"Yeah, well, he got sick last year and I try to help out as much as I can."

"I'm sorry to hear that. He's lucky to have you."

A lull of silence fell over us, and another shopper was trying to get by the aisle.

"Well, I'll see you around," she said, pushing her cart around the corner.

I continued shopping and tried focusing on my list, but I couldn't help looking for her down every aisle. There was something about her I really liked. I spotted her a few times, but I didn't want her to actually think I was a stalker, so I pretended not to notice her.

A few days later, as I was waiting in the long line for my iced coffee at Dunkin, I saw her in line a few people ahead of me. It wasn't hard to spot her with that fiery red hair. After I ordered, I moved to wait for the barista to call my name. Bridget hadn't noticed me yet. I stepped next to her and she looked up at me when she sensed my presence.

"I promise I'm really not stalking you," I chuckled, putting my hands up in defense.

"I'm really starting to question that. First my park. Then my grocery store. Then my coffee shop."

"*Yours?*"

"I was here first. You're in my territory."

I laughed.

"I'm willing to share, though."

I liked the sound of that.

"So, do you live around here?" I asked.

"Don't you already know where I live?"

I looked at her questioningly.

She smirked. "That's usually the first thing a stalker finds out."

"Ha ha," I said sarcastically.

"I live down the block."

"Me too. My building is on Seventh."

"Well, then I'm sure I'll be seeing you around."

"Lucky me." I grinned.

She rolled her eyes and then the barista called her name. She gave me a little wave before walking up to the counter and grabbing her coffee. She said a quick thank you and left a tip in the jar before walking out the door.

I liked knowing I would be bumping into her more now that I knew we lived close to each other. It felt like I'd made a friend besides Kenny. Well, an acquaintance was probably a better way to describe it. A good-looking acquaintance at that.

The rest of the week and weekend went by and I didn't see her again. I was a little disappointed, but three times in a few days was pretty lucky. The following Monday, I went to the grocery store at the same time as before, but I didn't see her there.

After I unpacked my groceries and put them away, I sat in my office for a video call with a potential investor. My father had set the meeting up with one of his friends who had more money than he knew what to do with. I wondered why my dad would throw me such a good bone. Was it out of the kindness of his own heart? Doubtful.

The meeting lasted for an hour, and I must have made a good impression because by the end I was sending over an agreement. It was a huge account. After I hung up, I called my dad.

"Hello?" He picked up on the third ring.

"Hey, Dad."

"Well, how did it go?" he asked.

"He signed with me. I'm overseeing all of his investments."

"Good. Now don't mess this up now, okay? I put a lot on the line for this meeting."

Way to have faith, Dad.

"I won't. I appreciate you doing that for me."

"I didn't do it *for* you. I did it because I wanted to earn his trust for another business opportunity I have. He's a real family man, so I wanted to prove that I was, too."

Wow. There it was. The real reason.

"Well, thanks anyway," I said, trying to hide my annoyance.

"Again, don't mess it up."

"I gotta go. Tell Mom I said hi." I hung up before he could say goodbye.

I was not going to let him ruin my mood, not after I had landed such a big account. I had to follow Kenny's advice and not let him get to me. It didn't matter how it came about; I had proved myself capable in that meeting. I was going to celebrate tonight.

I texted Kenny: *Landed a big account today. Celebrating tonight!*

Kenny: *That's awesome, man. I wish I could join you, but Cleo and I have dinner plans.*

Of course they did. Every night was date night when you were in the honeymoon stage.

Me: *No worries. Another time. Tell Cleo I said hey.*

At 7 p.m., I decided to go out solo. I knew just the place. Murphy's. At least there would be one familiar face to talk to. I spent a little longer getting ready, since the last few times I had run into Bridget I had been caught off guard. I chose a pair of jeans, a black T-shirt, and sprayed a little more cologne than normal. I called an Uber and rode the quick ten minutes to the bar. I figured I would have more than one drink tonight, so it was safer to Uber.

When I got out of the car, I suddenly felt a little nervous. Even though I had spent some time alone with Bridget, it still felt a little weird showing up to her place of work by myself. I found a high-top near the bar. Andy brought over menus and I ordered a whiskey on the rocks. I didn't see Bridget yet. She must have been in the back.

As I enjoyed my drink, I noticed a raven-haired woman eyeing me from across the bar. I gave her a slight smile as not to be awkward or rude, but it wasn't really an invitation. Although she took it that way. She slowly made her way over.

"Are you here all by yourself?" she asked, looking at the empty seat across from me.

"I'm waiting for a friend," I lied.

"Can I keep you company in the meantime?"

"Sure."

"I'm Simone," she said, sitting across from me.

"Justin."

She was pretty. Dark brown eyes. Nice smile. Low-cut top. She was the kind of woman I would take home normally, especially on a night like this when I was celebrating. But tonight, I wasn't feeling it.

I half listened as she told me about her job as a stylist at the large department store downtown. I waved down Andy for another drink. As I smiled and nodded, I felt someone's eyes on me. I looked around and spotted Bridget at the bar, smirking at me. How long had she been there?

I pretended my phone buzzed in my pocket and pulled it out to study the screen.

"Oh, you know what? My friend is on his way. It's been nice talking to you."

Simone looked at me disappointedly before grabbing her drink and leaving quickly. I grabbed my whiskey and headed to the bar where Bridget was pouring beer into pint glasses.

"Hi again," she said, making sure to fill the glass to the top.

"Hi." I sat down on a barstool.

"Where's your friend?" she asked, looking around.

"Kenny's not here tonight."

"No, your other friend. The one with the pretty smile."

"Oh, she's not with me."

"They just flock to you, don't they?" she asked, putting the pint glasses on a tray.

"I don't know about that."

"Don't look now, but another one's coming." She looked behind me expectantly.

I quickly turned around, but no one was there. She was messing with me.

"Ha ha," I said, rolling my eyes.

Bridget winked at me as she expertly balanced the tray of beer and walked it over to a table of customers. The rest of the evening, I found little moments to talk to her. I was happy it wasn't too busy, and she didn't seem to mind me sitting at the bar with her.

"Your friend with the nice smile is giving me the death stare," said Bridget at one point.

I shrugged. I didn't care.

"She seemed nice enough."

"I guess."

"What? Are you trying to tell me you're not *that* guy?" She raised an eyebrow.

"No. I am. Usually."

"Wow. Maybe Boston has changed you. Soon, you'll be settling down like your best friend, Kenny."

I quickly shook my head. "Nah."

"What? You don't want to be wifed up?"

"Hell no."

She nodded knowingly before turning her back and grabbing a bottle of liquor from the back shelf. I looked down into my drink. I had just convinced her that I *was* that guy. I didn't know why, but it made me feel a little guilty.

Chapter 7

Bridget

After Justin left the bar tonight, surprisingly alone, I couldn't stop thinking about what he said. He seemed like he could be with anyone. I had been witness to his effect on women here at the bar the past few times he had been in here. Of course, he was easy on the eyes, but he also had this quiet confidence about him. Except with me he was totally corny. A confident, cool, cornball. The three C's.

Even though he could have his choice of women, he had no interest in settling down. He made that known tonight when he practically shuddered at the thought. Maybe he was the typical guy I had assumed him to be. For some reason I felt a little let down by that, which was silly. It wasn't like I saw a future with the guy. I hardly knew him, but there was still something in him that I liked.

I also couldn't quite shake the feeling that maybe we were supposed to be in each other's lives in some way. There was no way we would run into each other as many times as we had the past week and not have it mean something. Truthfully, I found myself disappointed when I didn't see him at the park or the coffee shop again, which was why I was happy to see him walking through the doors of my bar tonight.

I wondered if he thought I was the typical girl looking for a man to settle down with and have their babies. Probably. The truth was, I was a lot like him. I had no interest in being wifed up and staying home with the kids. Sure, I felt lonely sometimes. Okay, a lot of the times. But the bar was my dream. It always had been. A relationship and kids didn't really work into the equation of working until 4 a.m. almost every night.

My relationships in the past hadn't worked out because of how much time I spent at Murphy's. My boyfriends were weirdly jealous of the place. And no, it wasn't the fact that as a bartender I was sometimes hit on. They were jealous of how much I worked and how little time I made for them.

"Who was that guy?" asked Andy, breaking me from my thoughts. He leaned against the counter next to me looking at the doors Justin had just walked out of.

"Oh, just a guy I met through Cleo. An acquaintance really."

"He's in here a lot."

"He's a fan of the fish and chips," I said nonchalantly.

"He's a fan of something." Andy wiggled his eyebrows.

I smacked him in the arm with the bar towel I had on my shoulder.

"What?" he asked with a laugh. "He's clearly into you."

"He's into anything with two legs and a vagina."

"Not true. I saw him turn down a raven-haired beauty tonight to come and talk to you."

"Big whoop." I twirled my finger in the air.

"Look, I know we don't know each other that well. I'm no Cleo, but I'm good to talk to about this kind of stuff."

"What stuff?" I asked, crinkling my nose.

"Relationship stuff."

"You're like twelve."

Andy was ten years younger than me. I wasn't sure what sort of advice he could possibly have for me. He was sweet and a good bartender, but that was about it.

"Just think about it," he said, pushing off the counter to take a customer's order.

I shook my head and began drying glasses that had just come out of the dishwasher. I noticed the guy who had been in here with Cara at a back table, sipping on a drink. I instantly got a bad feeling. I wondered how long he had been here. I wanted to confront him and ask him why he was staking the place out. I knew Cara wasn't going to give me any answers.

As I was about to walk over, one of my regulars plopped down in front of me. He looked all "woe is me," so I played therapist and bartender for the next fifteen minutes. When I had a chance to break away, the guy in the suit was gone.

"Hey Andy," I called.

"What's up, boss?" he asked.

"Do you know who that guy was? Table ten."

"No, he didn't say much. Paid with cash."

"Thanks." I nodded.

The next morning, I woke up around nine and headed to the coffee shop. I was running on only four hours of sleep, but I had admin work to get done at the bar. I needed all the caffeine I could get. As I stood in line, I saw none other than Justin a few people ahead of me. Of course. I looked down at my sweats and baggy T-shirt. I tightened the messy bun I had twisted on the top of my head. Could I be any less hot? I kept my head down, hoping he wouldn't see me.

I breathed a sigh of relief when he walked out the door after I ordered my coffee. He hadn't seen me. But I had seen him. He looked good. Guys in suits weren't normally my thing, but on him, it did something for me. I leaned against a partition and waited for my name to be called.

"Bridget? Order for Bridget," the barista called out.

I walked up and reached for my coffee, and my hand brushed against someone else's as they reached across the counter.

"Oh, sorry," I said, looking up and seeing Justin smiling at me.

"Hi," he said.

"I thought you left," I blurted out.

He raised an eyebrow.

"I mean, I only thought I saw you, but I—"

He laughed. He wasn't buying it.

I snatched my coffee from the counter quickly. I felt my cheeks burning red.

"You weren't going to say hi?" he asked amused.

"It was a long night," I murmured, looking down at my clothes.

As if reading between the lines, he said, "I think you look pretty."

If my cheeks weren't red before, they were sure to be now. This handsome guy decked out in a suit had no business calling me pretty.

"Liar," I muttered. I fought back a smile as I took a sip of my coffee.

Justin checked his watch.

"Shoot, I have to go. I'm late for my meeting. It was good to see you, Bridget." He awkwardly put his hand on my shoulder and looked me in the eye. His eyes were a deep greyish blue. I hadn't noticed that before. I quickly looked away and down at his hand that was suddenly sending warmth through my entire body. He gave me a little squeeze and then headed for the door. Did he just feel that too? A surge of electricity. I was awake now, and it wasn't the coffee.

At the bar, it was just me. Everyone else was home, probably asleep or getting rest for their shifts tonight. I posted up behind the counter and began going through receipts. I wanted everything filed away correctly before the busy weekend ahead. As I filed everything, I wondered if Justin would stop by again. I hoped he would.

Just then, the door to the bar opened.

"Sorry, we're closed," I said, internally scolding myself for not locking the door.

"Hey Bridg."

I looked up and saw Cara at the door. She gave me a little wave and walked toward me with a smile that looked more nervous than genuine.

"Cara. What are you doing here?"

"I tried your place, but you weren't home."

"I have a thing called a phone, you know. You could try calling it."

"Uh yeah, I don't know where my phone is at the moment." She took a seat on a barstool.

I shook my head as I continued filing receipts. She was seriously a child. She'd probably lose her head if it wasn't attached. She cleared her throat.

"What do you need, Cara?" I put the receipts down on the counter.

"Why do you think I need something?" she asked innocently.

I glared at her.

"Okay. I need some money."

"Wait, I feel like I'm having déjà vu here. Didn't we just do this whole thing?"

"I know, I know. I don't need ten grand though. Anything will help. I just need two grand."

"Oh, sure. I have two grand in the back. Let me go get it for you."

"Really?" she asked, surprised.

"No, Cara. Not really. Why the hell do you need so much money?"

Cara huffed loudly and sat back. She glared at me and muttered under her breath. I strained my ears to hear. I thought I heard her say something about interest.

"What did you say?"

"Nothing," she snapped.

"Cara, I just want to know what's going on."

"And I just want my big sister to help me out for once!" Cara slammed her hands on the counter, causing receipts to fly everywhere. She stood abruptly and walked out the door of the bar.

I sat behind the bar in shock. My breath was shaky. I was practically seething. After a few minutes, my anger turned to worry. Two feelings I often associated with my sister. Right now, I had to push my feelings aside. There was work to do.

As much as I wanted answers from my sister, my life couldn't revolve around her right now. I looked down at the floor and began picking up the receipts that had scattered. I finished filing everything, despite how hard it was to focus, and headed home.

The rest of the weekend passed by in a blur. Cara didn't come back to the bar. And to my disappointment, neither did Justin. I found myself distracted and short with customers, which was the last thing I wanted to be as the bar's owner. This was why I distanced myself from my sister because her problems eventually took over my life. By the time I got home in the early hours of Sunday morning, I passed out face-down on my bed still in my bar clothes.

I ended up dreaming about being tangled up in thorny vines. Every time I tried to break free, they tightened their grip on me, digging deep into my skin. I felt like I was suffocating and then I saw it. A red, scaly dragon making its way toward me through the forest. I tried to scream, but nothing came out. The vines grew tighter around my arms and legs. When the dragon was about to strike, I tried to shut my eyes, but dreams didn't work that way.

Suddenly, I saw a sword come crashing down, leaving a gash in the dragon's neck. I looked frantically around and saw Justin fighting through the vines, wielding a giant silver sword. The dragon turned away from me to face its attacker. I watched as Justin drew the dragon away from me, fighting it off with his sword. I could feel the vines loosening their grip. I broke free and that was when I woke up.

I rolled over onto my back, breathing heavy. I ran my hands up my arms to see if the vines were still wrapped around me, but they weren't. I wasn't in a forest. There was no dragon. There was no Justin. I was in my room, in my bed. Safe.

I rubbed my eyes gruffly as I looked around my room. That was one of the most vivid dreams I'd had in a while. I hardly remembered my dreams, but that one was going to stick with me. My mom used to always say that dreams meant something, especially when they were so clear. But what did it mean? I couldn't help but wonder that maybe Justin was really meant to be in my life. Maybe he was there to help me in some way. With what? I didn't know, but I was going to make it a point to talk to him as soon as I could.

Chapter 8

Justin

I paced the sidewalk outside the bar as my mom chattered away on the phone. I had wrapped up my meetings for the day and had walked over to Murphy's for a late lunch. It had seemingly become my local hangout. My spot when I needed a release. I liked the cozy pub. It was relaxed, cheap, and the bar's owner wasn't so bad either. I had been here now at least once a week. If only I could get in there now. I hadn't expected my mom to call today. I loved her, but she worried too much. And today, she was talking too much.

"Justin, are you there?"

"Yeah, Mom. I'm here." I rubbed the back of my head impatiently.

"I'm just worried about you, honey."

"Mom, I'm a grown man."

"You're still my baby." She sounded like she was on the verge of tears.

"What are you so worried about?"

"I don't know. Boston. It doesn't suit you."

"How so? You haven't even come to visit me once."

"You know how I am with traveling."

I scoffed. "You were just in Greece."

"That's different. That was for your aunt's birthday." Right. Logical. I rolled my eyes.

"Why don't you come visit, Mom? You can see my place. I can take you around the city. You'd like it."

She was quiet for a moment.

"Mom?"

"You don't even have an office, honey." She ignored my invitation.

I should have known my dad was behind this call, feeding her with doubt about my career choice.

"And?"

"It just seems strange. To leave your big office here in New York, let alone your family, and go to a new city to what? Work from your condo?"

"Mom, plenty of people work remote these days. You know that. You make it seem like I'm doing nothing all day." I shook my head. She and my dad were both so old-fashioned and stuck in their ways. They had difficulty believing someone could be successful working in a way that was foreign to them.

"I just think you're better suited for New York. You know, with a *real* job."

"I have a *real* job, Mom. I've started my own advising firm. You know that."

"Well, your dad said you still had a job here if you wanted it."

"But I don't want it. I want something that's my own. Why is that so hard to understand?"

I glanced at my watch. We had been on the phone for nearly forty-five minutes, just doing this back-and-forth thing. This was taking longer than I had anticipated and I was growing more annoyed by the minute.

I loved my mom very much. She and I had always gotten along. Despite her and my dad being stuck in their ways, she was usually more understanding than my father. She was warmer too. She actually felt like a parent, whereas my dad felt like a boss. Still, every so often, he pressured her into talking to me about whatever I wasn't listening to him about. Usually, she softened me to whatever ideas my dad had put in her head, but not this time.

I heard my mom sigh on the other line. I might as well finish this conversation with a pint glass in hand. A smile from Bridget wouldn't hurt either. I walked to the door and pulled it open. I blinked a few times as I stepped inside, trying to adjust my eyes to the dim lighting. It was lunchtime, so the place wasn't busy. I liked coming when it was slow because it meant more time to talk to Bridget uninterrupted. I could hear my mom talking on the other line, but I wasn't paying much attention anymore.

I held my phone against my cheek with my shoulder as I looked around the bar. I spotted

Bridget behind the counter. She was wiping the countertops and looked lost in thought. She wore her usual jeans and Murphy's tee. Her hair was pulled back in a claw clip, but the front of her red hair fell around her face. Her brows were slightly furrowed as she worked at a spot on the counter with a rag. I admired her for a second. She really was beautiful. I wondered if she knew that.

"Justin? Are you there?" my mom asked impatiently on the other line.

"Yes. Still here."

"Look, I'll think about making a trip, okay? Just don't tell your father."

Bridget looked up and caught my eye. She looked surprised. She stopped what she was doing and tossed the rag on the counter. She saw my phone and made a slashing motion with her hand as if to end the call. Weird, but okay. I'd be happy to.

"Hey, Mom. I have to go."

"Wait, what? Justin…"

"Sorry. Love you, bye."

"Just think about moving home," I heard her say as I hit the end button.

I walked toward the bar and looked at Bridget curiously. She eyed me almost nervously. I wondered what was going on. I took a seat in front of her as she slid me a beer. I looked up at her questioningly.

"It looked like you needed it." She shrugged. Her eyes left mine quickly, as if avoiding my gaze. She wasn't her usual confident, cocky self.

"Thanks," I said as I picked it up and took a long sip. The frosted glass felt cool in my hands and the beer ran down my throat with ease. I let out a comforted sigh as I leaned back in the bar stool.

"Everything okay?" she asked, looking down at her hands as she fumbled her fingers.

"Peachy." I took another long sip of beer. I might as well down it, so I did. Nothing like a little beer to numb the bullshit.

Why did I let my mother get to me that way? Especially when I knew my father had put her up to it. It was the same old song and dance. Still, she somehow always persuaded me or at least got under my skin.

I had no intention of moving back home. Still, part of me felt guilty for disappointing my mom. I had found my footing in Boston without the watchful eye of my father. I did it on my own, and I was building something that was my own. I knew that pissed off my father. He liked feeling like I was under his finger. He liked feeling like I owed him something.

Sure, he had pushed me to go to his university. He had pushed me into a career in finance. He had so graciously offered me a job at his financial firm, and reminded me of it nearly every day. How he had taken a chance on me and how I had to prove myself being the boss's son. I owed him a lot, but not everything. I had worked my ass off to build a reputable clientele. I deserved this chance on my own, in a new city. I deserved to prove that I didn't need him and that I could do things my way.

I realized I had been lost in thought for longer than appropriate, holding an empty beer glass in my hands. I shook my head as if to clear my mind. I placed the glass on the counter a little more aggressively than I intended, causing Bridget to jump a little.

"Sorry," I muttered, shaking my head.

"What is it?" she asked.

"Family stuff," I grumbled.

"I know all about that. Trust me." She nodded knowingly as she placed her hand on mine and gave me a squeeze. It felt weirdly intimate. Bridget usually had a tough exterior, one that I often tried to break through. When I did break through, the little glimpses I got of her were like rays of light pouring through holes in a wall. A pretty wall, for that matter.

I glanced up at her and her green eyes looked deep and understanding. She held her gaze for only a moment before I felt her hand twitch around mine. She quickly pulled it away, as if she had touched a hot stove. She let out a little nervous laugh as she tucked a strand of hair behind her ear.

What was up with her? I studied her curiously. She had moved away from the counter as if keeping her distance. Her hands were shoved in her back pockets and she was chewing on her bottom lip. Those lips. I had trouble not staring at them, wondering what they tasted like. Imagining my teeth around them. I tore my gaze away and raised a questioning eyebrow.

She stood quiet for a moment. I was not prepared for what came next.

"Will you have sex with me?" she blurted out. She looked around to make sure no one heard her before returning her gaze to me. She was fully serious.

Whoa. That was not what I was expecting to come out of her mouth. I felt my eyes widen. Women had given me the proposition of sex before, and I'd often eagerly accepted. They were a lot less direct about it though. It was more like a hand on the arm, or a foot grazing up my leg, or leaning in as they pushed their breasts together. They had never come right out and asked me. It had never been from a beautiful redhead with a strong will either. I was out of my element here.

I blinked a few times, trying to hide my surprise.

"I know that's such a weird thing to ask. I hardly know you. You hardly know me," she rambled. She began to pace behind the back of the bar.

"It's just I'm stressed. So stressed. I have so much on my plate. And my dreams. God, my dreams. You've been in them. Fighting dragons.

Saving me. From what? I don't know. My mom always said dreams mean something…" she continued rambling. I wondered if she was even talking to me anymore, or just lost in her thoughts. I tried my best to keep up.

"Dragons?" I asked, trying to get a grasp.

She stopped her frantic pacing and placed her palms on the counter, looking at me seriously.

"I need sex, and it needs to be you," she said sternly.

I pretended to think about it seriously. My answer was *yes*. A *hell yes*. I knew that right when she blurted the question out, but I didn't want to give myself away too quickly.

"Can you get me another beer, please?" I asked.

She looked taken aback for a second before nodding and taking my glass from the counter. She held it under the spout and slowly, expertly filled it to avoid foam. She slid it across the counter to me. She leaned against the back counter with her arms crossed, clearly waiting for my answer. I casually took a sip of my beer.

"Yes," I said after a moment.

"Yes? Really?" she asked, raising her eyebrows.

"Why not?" I shrugged.

She sucked in a breath and nodded slowly as if processing what she herself had proposed. "Okay," she said quietly.

"Okay." I said, taking another sip of my beer.

"Okay," she said again. More confident this time.

I watched as Bridget suddenly dragged a stepstool to a stack of nearby shelves. She stepped up and reached for a bottle of tequila on the top shelf. She held it carefully as she stepped down and set it on the counter in front of her. She grabbed a shot glass and filled it to the top. She downed it and let out a gasp. She ducked under the counter and grabbed my hand, tugging me to follow her.

"Let's go." She nodded toward a staircase at the back of the bar that I hadn't noticed before.

"Wait. We're doing this now?" I trailed behind her in shock.

Chapter 9

Bridget

"Andy, can you cover for me?" I called out.

He looked up and nodded at me curiously. I was grateful it was a slow afternoon. I wondered what he was thinking as he watched me drag a guy I barely knew through the bar with me. I didn't wake up this morning thinking, "Hey, today feels like a good day to ask a practical stranger for sex." But when Justin walked into the bar this afternoon, and I saw his dark eyes watching me, I started feeling something bubbling up inside of me.

I had been thinking about that damn dream for days, trying to figure out what it meant. What did I need saving from and why was Justin the one to come to my rescue? Nothing really pieced together in a way that made sense. I wasn't entirely sure that sex was the subconscious root of the dream. I was actually pretty positive that wasn't the dream's meaning, but here he was looking sexy as hell in my bar.

Still, the words tumbled out of me before I could grab a hold of them. Now his hand was in mine, following me upstairs. I figured there was no time like the present. Plus, I didn't want him to change his mind. The less thinking about it the better. Thinking and talking about it would only complicate things, and right now I just needed a release that I was sure he would give to me.

We reached the top of the stairs and stood in silence as I pulled a ring of keys from my pocket. I could hear him breathing behind me. He was close enough to where his breath landed softly against my neck, making the hairs on my arm stand up. I unlocked the door swiftly and pushed it open.

Most people didn't know this little loft was up here. It used to be my dad's office until I took over. Having slept here more than a few times when I didn't want to drive home, I decided to make the space a bit more cozy. I added a velvet green couch underneath the small paned window, a little wooden table with a stack of books on top, and a full-sized bed centered against the back wall.

I held the door as Justin strode past me and stopped in the center of the room. I gently closed the door, the sounds of the bar muffled to a silence. I could feel my heart racing in my chest. Justin looked around the room. I studied him for a moment. He was wearing a pair of black sweats and a black shirt that fit snug against his broad shoulders. His silver hair contrasted with his tan skin and dark clothing. Something took over me.

A burning longing. I took a deep breath and a few determined steps toward him.

He turned to face me. "I didn't know this was up—"

Before he could finish, I lifted onto my tiptoes and pressed my lips against his harshly. He stumbled slightly, regaining his balance by gripping my hips. I pressed my body into his, pushing him toward the couch, my lips never leaving his. His knees crumpled as they met the couch and he was forced to sit back. I climbed on top of him, straddling him, and looked down.

He looked up at me, clearly surprised. "Are you sure about this?" he asked.

Rather than answer him, I brought my lips to his once more. I ran my tongue against his smooth lips, parting them so I could enter his mouth. His tongue met mine gently at first, and then with more ferocity. I felt him let out a deep breath as the tension left his body. I gripped the back of the couch and positioned myself firmly against him.

As if he got the go- ahead, he lifted one hand to the back of my neck while his other hand trailed to my lower back. He gathered my hair in his hand and pulled, our lips breaking apart as I looked up at the ceiling. I let out a small, audible gasp. His lips were suddenly on my neck, gently kissing me from my collarbone to behind my ear. I felt myself shiver. He ran his tongue back down to where my shirt lay just above my breasts.

He breathed against me as his other hand trailed up my back, under my shirt, and found the clasp to my bra. With ease, he pinched the clasp until it broke free. I slid my hands under the sleeves of my shirt and unlooped the straps from my arms, pulling it out from under my shirt, and tossing it aside. He gave me a sly smile as he released my hair and trailed his hands down the sides of my body until his fingers met the bottom of my shirt. I met his gaze and lifted my arms above my head.

His hands moved slowly, almost torturingly, as he lifted my shirt up and over my head. My breasts spilled out before him and I watched as he took them in hungrily with his eyes. Him wanting me made me want him more. He tore his gaze away from my breasts and met my eyes. Never breaking his gaze, he took my breasts into his mouth, one by one. He trailed his tongue against my nipples, causing me to arch my back with pleasure. He continued sucking on them as he kneaded my breasts with his large hands.

I could feel him growing hard against me. Even through my jeans, which I regretted wearing, I could feel the size of him. There was too much fabric separating us. As if reading my mind, he pulled his mouth away from me and ran his hands up my thighs. Suddenly, he lifted me off him and tossed me on the couch with ease. I looked up at him expectantly. He clambered over me and his fingers fiddled with the button on my jeans. He undid the button and pulled the zipper slowly down. His hands gripped the waistband of my jeans and shimmied them off my legs. He tossed them on the floor and stood up, looking at me from head to toe. I could feel myself growing wet against my black mesh panties.

I caught his gaze and bit my lip slightly as I parted my legs. His eyes slowly trailed down to my panties. His breathing grew heavier as I spread my legs even more.

"Jesus, Bridget," he whispered before grabbing my hips and pulling me to the edge of the couch. He hovered over me, bringing his lips to mine. Our tongues lashed against each other frantically, and then reduced down to a slow, rhythmic dance. His one hand steadied him against the couch, as the other began to explore. He trailed his fingers across my navel and down my inner thighs. Soon they traveled slowly back up and met the black mesh of my panties.

He put his forehead to mine and watched me as he lightly grazed against me. I shuddered at his touch, but didn't break our gaze. His fingers began to rub against me harder and faster. I could feel myself growing wetter through the mesh. I knew he could feel it too, because his lips were pressed into a small smile. I lifted my hips slightly because I needed more. He delivered by gently pulling the mesh aside and running his finger over my bare clit. With ease, he dipped his finger into me slowly. Deliciously. I let out a small moan as he pulled his finger away and entered me more vigorously.

My hands were buried in his hair. My eyes intent on his. My breath heavy against his mouth that was inches away from mine. My hips moved rhythmically against his hand. Soon, he pulled his face from mine as he lowered onto his knees in front of me, his fingers gently holding me open. I watched his eyes meet mine. They were needy. Wanting. He trailed his pinky against me as he moaned. I felt his warm breath as his tongue lapped. My eyes involuntarily closed as I took the sensation in. His tongue and fingers moved in beautiful unison as I tried to keep my hips still. Breathy moans escaped my throat as he moved his tongue against me. My hands tugged at his hair, bringing him closer to me. I felt myself close to the edge, and I hadn't even tasted him yet. I hadn't even felt his girth inside me. I breathlessly pulled him away from me.

He kneeled in front of me as he licked his lips. God, he was hot. I sat up and reached for his shirt. I tugged on it, lifting it over his head and revealing his tight muscles underneath. I took him in for a moment before I stood up, pulling him with me. I tilted my head up and he brought his mouth down to mine. I took his bottom lip between my teeth and my hand grazed against his erection. He let out a groan as his eyes rolled back.

I guided him carefully backward toward the bed and pushed him down onto the mattress.

He watched me expectantly as I reached for the waistband of his sweats. I pulled them off with ease, followed by his briefs, releasing his hard cock. I swallow hard as I took him in, and the desire took hold of me even more. I climbed up toward him, hovering my mouth directly above him. I meet his gaze as I swirled my tongue against his tip, tasting him. I felt his body hitch and watched as his eyes closed.

I trailed my tongue down his shaft slowly, and back up toward the tip before opening my mouth and take him in completely. He reached his hands to grasp my face as he throbbed inside my mouth. I moved slowly at first and then faster. His hands moved to the bedsheets and grasped them tightly. I slid my gaze up to him and he gave me a look of utter want. Slowly, I pulled my mouth away from him and climbed up his body, straddling him. I lowered myself against him.

I slid myself against his shaft, feeling every inch of him without taking him in. I was teasing him and it felt delicious. I grinded slowly against him, watching him begin to lose control. Finally, he did. He grabbed my hips and lifted them into the air, holding me steady as he pressed his tip to my ready opening. I felt myself open up wider as he slowly eased me onto him, every tantalizing inch filling me.

I let out a loud gasp as he gripped my hips and grinded me against his cock that was buried inside of me. I threw my head back and continued riding him as he hit me in all the right places. Suddenly, he lifted me up without ever leaving me and pressed my back against the bed. I spread my legs wide as he began thrusting inside of me, faster and faster. I stretched even further as he pounded into me, his hands gripping the flesh of my outer thighs. I watched as his eyes closed and his head tilted back, simultaneous with my loss of control. My body began to shake as he moaned loudly, his cock throbbing and filling me.

We lay there for a moment, completely breathless. I stared up at the ceiling, him still inside me. He groaned as he rolled off me and lay next to me. I let out a satisfied sigh. That had been everything I needed and more. Maybe this was why I needed him. A momentary stress relief, nothing more. Besides, he wasn't that kind of guy, and I didn't need him to be.

Chapter 10

Justin

Bridget lay next to me, blinking slowly as she stared up at the ceiling. I was trying to catch my breath, still wrapping my head around what had just happened. Whatever that was. It was desperate. Maybe careless. Definitely good. So good. Best sex of my life, no doubt.

I rolled onto my side and brushed my lips against her bare shoulder. She turned slowly and gave me a small smile. I wondered what she was thinking. I couldn't read her. I hoped she was pondering round two.

Suddenly, she pushed the sheets off her and climbed out of bed. I propped myself on my elbows and watched her naked body cross the room. *Wow*, I thought, as she strode away from the bed. Her skin was soft and creamy. A stark contrast to her bright auburn hair that hung in loose waves down her back. I wanted more than anything for her to climb back in.

Instead, she searched for her clothes by the little green couch across the room where we had started. She grabbed her clothes from the floor, trying to cover herself as she found her way to a small door in the corner of the room. She stepped in, closing the door behind her. I heard a toilet flush and a sink run. After a few minutes, she came out fully clothed.

"Leaving already?" I asked.

"I have to get back," she said, finally looking at me as if she remembered I was there.

I guessed that was that. I lay back and put my hands behind my head. I chewed on the inside of my cheek. I felt a little stunned lying there by myself as Bridget slid her shoes on before she strode toward me.

Soon she was standing over me, putting her hair up into a ponytail. She leaned down and gave me a quick kiss on the lips.

"Thank you for that," she said, eyeing me up and down.

Then she was gone. She walked out the door and back down to the bar. She had left in such a hurry. I couldn't help but feel a little used.

Normally, that wouldn't bother me. Not that this has ever happened before. First, a woman had never propositioned me for sex in such a verbally direct manner. Second, a woman had never dipped out as quickly as Bridget had just now. I didn't feel self-conscious about my skills in the bedroom. I know we both enjoyed it. There was no faking that.

Maybe we should have talked about it, but I was under the impression talking was not what she wanted. There was no chance to, anyway. The second we got up here, her lips were on mine and there was no protesting that. There was a sense of urgency to the whole thing. I almost felt like I was her life support in some way.

There was nothing quick about our time together though. I closed my eyes and replayed our moments on the couch and moving to the bed. It was the best sex of my life. Then she was gone. Back to work downstairs. I didn't think it was that busy that she needed to hurry and get back.

I lay there a little longer, lost in my thoughts. Why was I so in my head about this? I just got laid by a beautiful girl I had been eyeing ever since I met her a few weeks ago. I didn't get in my feelings like this. It wasn't like I wanted a serious relationship, and she knew that. I made that pretty clear when I physically shuddered at the idea of settling down. Maybe we were the same. Maybe she wasn't looking for anything serious either. This could be a win-win situation. I should be happy.

I sighed and sat up, scanning the floor for my clothes. I had better get out of here before things got any more awkward. I untangled myself from the sheets and grabbed my sweats and shirt, pulling them both on. I ran my hand through my hair in an attempt to look presentable for my walk of shame, which I hoped no one would see. I opened the door of the loft quietly and slipped out. I walked swiftly down the stairs and breathed a sigh of relief to see Bridget and Andy both behind the bar drying glasses.

As I suspected, the bar only had a few customers. Not busy at all. I didn't want her to see me, let alone Andy, who probably had his assumptions about what just happened. I suddenly remembered a back exit just around the corner that I'd seen a service guy leave out of last week. I swiftly made my way to the door and pushed it open, exiting to the back alley. The sky was turning a shade of orangish pink. I checked my watch. It was nearing six. We had been up in that loft awhile. I smiled to myself.

On the drive home, I rolled the windows down and turned up the classic rock radio station, hoping it would get me out of my head. But when I got home, I went straight to my room and fell face-down on my bed. This whole thing, whatever it was with Bridget, was really bothering me.

I hadn't liked a girl like this in a while, and while I didn't think I was looking for a relationship, something about Bridget was different. I couldn't help thinking I had screwed up. This wasn't how things worked. Relationships were hardly borne out of one-night stands, or one-afternoon stands. If that was what that was. I hoped it wasn't. I wanted more than just one of that.

I wondered if I should have asked her out on a proper date. I had plenty of opportunities to. We had kept running into each other, and of course, I'd see her at the bar. Our conversations were always easy and I kept finding more and more to like about her.

I rolled over onto my back and shook my head. I couldn't wallow all night about this. I dug in my pocket for my phone. I scrolled through my contacts and texted Kenny:

Hey man.

Kenny: *Hey. What's up?*

Me: *Want to go out tonight?*

Kenny: *We're actually having a cookout. I was just going to text you.*

Me: *Be there soon. I'll bring beer.*

I locked my phone and tossed it on the bed. I'd practically had to force myself out. No, I wasn't going to be this guy. I was going to go out and get her off my mind. Wait. Kenny. Cleo. Bridget. What if she was there? I doubted it. It seemed like she never had a night off. I would be in the clear.

I hopped in the shower, letting the steam waft over me. The hot water washed away any trace Bridget had left behind. The smell of her perfume, her lips against mine, her hands in my hair… I shut the shower off abruptly. There wasn't time for that. I dried off with a towel and walked to my bedroom. I ordered an Uber as I threw on some jeans and a white tee. I was planning on numbing my feelings tonight.

Thirty minutes later, I arrived at Kenny's penthouse apartment, after I picked up a twelve-pack of craft beer on the way. I rode the elevator up fourteen stories until the doors opened to his massive entryway. The place was packed with players from the team and women. A lot of beautiful women.

"Justin!" Chad called out. He was the oldest player on the team, not that his age meant he was old in any way. For the major leagues, yeah, but he still acted like a kid.

"Hey, man," I said, patting him on the back.

"Glad you could make it. Where've you been?" he asked.

"Uh, I was working and then at Murphy's."

"Ahh, good ol' Murphy's. Was Bridget working?" he asked, raising his brows hopefully.

I forgot Chad had a major thing for her. Was that a little tinge of jealousy I was feeling?

"Yeah." I shrugged casually.

"God, she is my dream girl." Chad sighed.

"Well, good to see you, man. Where is Kenny?"

Chad nodded toward the kitchen. I clutched the pack of beer and made my way through the crowd to the kitchen. It was huge. White marble counters with black matte cabinets surrounded the entirety of the kitchen. It had two stacked ovens and two chef-sized refrigerators. This was even bigger than his last one. It made sense, though. He was engaged to Cleo. She was the newest and hottest pastry chef in Boston.

I opened the large beer and wine fridge and began unpacking the beer, loading it into the fridge. I grabbed one before closing the door.

"Can you grab one for me, too?" asked Kenny as he walked toward me.

I nodded and handed him one.

"Thanks, man." He clinked his bottle to mine. "Glad you could make it."

"Thanks for the invite."

"Come on. Let's head up to the deck." He waved for me to follow him.

We climbed the spiral staircase in the center of the living room and came out on the rooftop deck to where the sun had just set, filling the sky with a swirl of pink and purple. The air was filled with the smell of grilled hot dogs and burgers. I realized just how hungry I was after my afternoon with Bridget.

"Hungry?" asked Kenny.

"Starved."

"Help yourself." He grabbed a plate from the large buffet table.

I loaded my plate with a hot dog, cheeseburger, potato salad, Caesar salad, and French fries.

"You weren't kidding," chuckled Kenny as he eyed my plate.

I laughed as I took a bite of my hot dog.

"So, what did you do today?" he asked, filling his plate with about half the amount of food I had.

"Oh, just the usual meetings. I did stop by Murphy's for lunch."

"You have your new spot. I knew you'd like it."

I nodded.

"Any new developments with Bridget?" he asked, wiggling his eyebrows.

"What? No," I answered a little too quickly. Kenny knew I was into her. We had known each other long enough that he could read me like a book.

He looked at me suspiciously.

"Okay, you can't say anything," I said under my breath.

"What?"

"She asked to have sex with me."

"Fuck off!" Kenny practically yelled. He didn't believe me. Why would he? "I'm serious. She just came right out and asked me."

He twisted his lips as if he was trying to determine if he should believe me or not. "And what did you say?"

"Well, obviously I said yes."

Kenny took a sip of his beer and shook his head. "So, when is your little date going to happen?"

I was quiet a moment. "It kind of already did. At the bar."

"What?" He nearly spit out his beer.

"She dragged me upstairs to the loft, and without a word, she came on to me."

"That doesn't sound like Bridget, but Cleo knows her better than I do."

"Trust me, I didn't see that coming."

He lifted an eyebrow. "And?"

"And what?"

"How was it?"

"Best. Sex. Ever," I said, pausing between each word for effect.

"Cheers to that." Kenny clinked his bottle against mine.

I took a sip of beer.

"What?" asked Kenny, eyeing me.

"I don't know. I just felt a little used. It's dumb, I know. I just got laid. So why do I feel so lousy?"

"Talk to Cleo. Maybe she can give you some insight."

"Yeah, good idea."

I sat down and finished my plate of food as Kenny talked to me about next season. I half listened as I scanned the rooftop for Chloe. I needed answers.

Chapter 11

Bridget

I finished pouring whiskey in a tumbler and slid it to the guy in front of me. He had been hitting on me all night and he was pretty easy on the eyes, but I was just flirting for the tips. I had no interest in him. Truthfully, I couldn't get my afternoon with Justin out of my head. It had been three days, but the images of him and me together wouldn't leave my mind. I felt my cheeks grow warm just thinking about it.

"Thanks, sweetheart," the guy said as he picked up his drink. His name was Brett. I think. I was only half listening.

"Of course," I said with a smile.

"So, you run this place all by yourself?"

"I do."

"Seems like a lot of work for someone as pretty as yourself."

I internally rolled my eyes. He was cute, but not a lot going on up there clearly.

"You'd be surprised by what I can do."

"I bet," he said as he looked me up and down. He took a sip of his drink.

"I better go tend to the rest of the bar. As much as I want to, I can't spend all night over here with you," I knocked my knuckles on the table and gave him a wink. It was all part of the act. My dad kept customers coming back with his loud, father-like hosting skills and his wide knowledge of baseball. I realized I kept customers coming back by making them think they had a chance. It wasn't my favorite, but it worked.

"I wish you could," I heard him call after me.

I was thankful it was a somewhat busy night, so I didn't have to. I took a customer's order and began making a tray of drinks for his table that was nearby. They wanted beer and shots. They must have been celebrating something. After I filled my tray, I carefully balanced it as I walked from out behind the bar. As I approached the table, I saw the door to the bar open. I had been watching it all night. The past few days even. Justin hadn't been back.

I was disappointed to see it wasn't him walking in, but a woman. Cara. I let out a small sigh of frustration before putting on a smile as I served the tray of drinks to the table.

"What are we celebrating tonight?" I asked, keeping my sister in the corner of my eye.

"I got a promotion!" one of the guys answered and the rest of the table cheered.

"Congratulations! This round is on me then."

They thanked me repeatedly as I walked back toward the bar where I saw my sister sitting sulkily on a barstool. I set the tray down loudly, causing her to jump.

"What do you need, Cara?" I asked shortly.

She chewed on her bottom lip. She honestly looked scared, which made me worried, but I tried to hide it. I needed to be strong. I had been down this road with Cara before, always getting her out of a jam and hoping it would be the last time she'd screw up. It never was. This time would probably be no different.

"Out with it. I have a business to run."

"I really need some money, sis."

"Are we seriously doing this again?"

"I don't understand why you can't just spot me some money. I'm good for it. I'll pay you back."

"Will you?" I raised an eyebrow.

"Yes! Bridget, trust me."

"Like the time I trusted you to take care of Dad when he first got sick? Or the time I trusted you to run the bar for one night? Or the time I lent you money to buy a car?"

When my dad first got sick, we had agreed that I would run the bar and she would take care of him. I ended up doing both. She never picked up his meds and I couldn't trust her to administer them on schedule. She didn't take care of the house, and instead used it as a place for friends to crash while my dad should have been getting rest.

When he was really sick one night, I wanted to stay with him and asked her to run the bar. It was a disaster. Even though I had given her a crash course and she had bartenders to help out, she called me almost every ten minutes with questions. Eventually, she gave up and the rest of the night she gave drinks away for free. We lost so much money that night and she kept all of the tips for her generosity, instead of putting it toward the bar.

Oh, and the money for the car disappeared and a car never appeared.

"It's different this time," she pleaded.

"When are you going to get your life together, Cara?"

"I'm trying. Not everyone can have the family business handed to them on a silver platter," she muttered.

I felt my face flush with anger. It took everything in me not to step out from behind the bar and yell in her face.

"I bought my share of this place. You know that. And I worked my ass off to prove that I belonged behind the bar," I said in a quiet rage. I didn't want to cause a scene.

Cara rolled her eyes like she was unconvinced.

"Cara, go home. Wherever that is. Don't come back here until you've got your life sorted out. I love you, but I have to do this for your own good." I reached for her hand, but she pulled it away.

"Don't use that big sister act on me. It's bullshit." She pointed her finger at me angrily. A few customers at the bar looked over curiously. I smiled at them, letting them know everything way okay.

"Cara. Go. Now," I said under my breath.

She stood from her barstool and pushed it away from her, causing it to tumble to the floor loudly. If we weren't causing a scene before, we surely were now.

"Sorry for intruding on your perfect life in your perfect bar. Dad always thought you were the perfect daughter," she practically yelled. Her body swayed slightly and her voice wavered with emotion. I started to wonder if she had been drinking. If she had been, it wasn't here at my bar. She had just gotten here.

"Cara, do you need me to call someone to get you?"

"Fuck off," she muttered as she walked to the door, pulling it open and then she was gone.

I let out a shaky breath. I felt a hand on my back. It was Andy looking at me worriedly.

"You okay?" he asked.

I gave him a little nod.

"Can you just make sure she's okay out there?" I asked.

"Of course."

I watched him as he disappeared out the door of the bar. I felt customers' eyes on me, but I ignored them. I tried to carry on like nothing had happened. After a few minutes, they realized the show was over and went back to enjoying their drinks. Andy came back inside.

"Well?"

"She didn't talk to me, but she let me order her an Uber."

"Thank you, Andy. I appreciate it."

"Of course. Family stuff is tough." He gave me a pat on the back and went to the other end of the bar where a customer was waving him down.

I leaned against the back of the bar to catch my breath. Part of me couldn't believe Cara had just come in here like that, but another part of me knew she could lose her head. The familiar anger and worry filled me. If it were any other person, I would cut them out of my life. This stress wasn't worth it. But she was my sister. I wrestled with my thoughts a little longer and then pulled out my phone.

I tried calling Cara, but it immediately went to voicemail. I stared at my phone for a minute longer and then scrolled through my contacts to Justin's name. He had given me his number a few visits back. I hesitated for a moment and then hastily sent him a text:

Hey. I need you. Can you come in to the bar tonight?

I watched the three dots appear. He was typing.

Justin: *Sure.*

I locked my phone and slid it into my back pocket. I should have been happy he was coming in, but instead I felt guilty. It didn't feel good to use someone, and that was what I was doing. That was what I had done a few days ago. Yes, it felt good. God, yes. I didn't realize how badly I needed that. But it wasn't right. Justin seemed like a nice enough guy. He didn't deserve this.

Plus, things could get messy. Sex felt good, but it often came with baggage. Even though he didn't want anything serious, and neither did I, it couldn't just be that simple. Someone, at some point, always wanted more.

I should just focus on the bar. This was my dream. A small part of me felt I should also focus on my sister. As much as she pissed me off, and as aggravating as tonight's encounter with her was, she needed me. No, I couldn't give her thousands of dollars, nor would I if I could. She didn't need money. She needed love and someone to point her in the right direction. In the past, I would always help her no questions asked. That got us both nowhere. Maybe this time a heart-to-heart would help.

"You okay, honey?" asked Brett, breaking me out of my thoughts.

I blinked a few times and brought myself back to the bar. I could focus on my sister later.

"Yeah, I'm fine." I smiled wide.

"Was that your sister?" he asked.

"Uh, yeah. How did you know?"

He pointed at his hair amused.

"Oh right, the red hair." Duh, I thought to myself.

"She's feisty."

"You have no idea." I shook my head.

"Does it run in the family?" He gave me a sly smile. I was not in the mood for this.

Just then, the door of the bar opened and I felt immediate relief at the sight of Justin standing in the doorway. Then I realized I was about to break things off. Whatever we had between us. I couldn't turn to him whenever I was stressed. That was not how life worked, and he didn't owe me anything.

He spotted me behind the bar and walked over.

"Hey, Justin!" Andy called out.

Justin raised his hand and greeted him. *When had those two become buddies?* I thought to myself. It was kind of cute. He took a seat next to Brett. Awkward.

"Hi," I said softly.

"Hi." He raised his eyebrow expectantly.

I was suddenly feeling very self-conscious. His hair was damp from the shower, and he wore a slouchy hoodie. He looked comfortably hot. I swallowed hard. Where had my confidence gone when I had blatantly asked him for sex? Maybe a shot of tequila would help.

Instead, I called to Andy, "Hey, can you watch the bar for a minute?"

Andy looked from me to Justin and tried not to smile. I gave him a glare that quickly wiped away his smile. While I didn't tell him what happened up in the loft, it wasn't hard to guess.

"You got it, boss." He cleared his throat nervously.

I ducked under the bar and reached for Justin's hand. His fingers intertwined in mine, and I thought I might throw up the butterflies in my stomach. Brett watched us with a furrowed brow as we started to walk away. I heard him mutter, "Lucky asshole" under his breath. I led Justin up the stairs to the loft. It felt all too familiar, except there was less urgency this time. And there would be no sex involved. I just needed to apologize.

Chapter 12

Justin

I followed Bridget up the familiar stairs to the loft. She wasn't pulling me where I had to keep up with her. Instead, my hand rested in hers gently and her grip was light. Something was different this time. She wasn't determined. Instead, she felt defeated. I wondered what was up.

I didn't know what to expect when her name popped up on my screen earlier tonight. I was eating a late dinner at home with no intention of going anywhere after a long day of work. Still, part of me was excited to see her name flash on the screen. I was even more excited that she wanted to see me again. Tonight.

We hadn't talked or seen each other since our afternoon together in this very loft she was leading me to. I had thought about texting or calling her, but I didn't have her number. She only had mine after I had given it to her. Sure, I could have asked Cleo for it, but I didn't want to seem too desperate.

After I got her text, I had quickly taken a shower and threw on some comfortable baggy clothes. I didn't want it to look like I had tried.

Still, seeing her tonight looking beautiful behind the bar made me wonder if an old college hoodie was the best choice for our rendezvous.

She unlocked the door and pushed it open, pressing against it to let me by. I walked into the room and stood with my hands in my pockets waiting for what was going to happen next. Was she going to basically attack me with her mouth again? Part of me hoped she would.

I watched as she closed the door to the loft. I noticed she didn't lock it this time. She turned around slowly and eyed me nervously. I raised my shoulders and looked around the room. Why did I feel so nervous this time?

She walked toward the green couch and sat down. I followed suit and sat beside her. We both started talking at the same time.

"So," she and I said in unison.

She let out a quiet laugh.

"You first," I said.

She nodded before taking a deep breath. "I'm sorry," she blurted out.

I jerked my head back in surprise and searched her face for why she would be apologizing.

"The other day was so out of character for me. I basically asked you for sex. No, I *did* ask you for sex. I can't believe I did that." She rubbed the palms of her hands against her cheeks in embarrassment.

"I don't know why I did that. I mean, it was great. *Really* great. Don't get me wrong. Like I can't stop thinking about it…" She was rambling now and I just let her go on because it was pretty cute to see her frantic this way.

"I just feel so bad about it. I need to find healthier ways to deal with stress than just ask some random hot guy to get me off. I mean, not that you're random *random*. I'm not totally crazy. I know you. Sort of. Cleo. Kenny. You know what I mean. I'm just so, so sorry."

She looked like she was about to continue or start crying, so I cut her off before she could worry herself even more. I grabbed her hands and held them tightly, catching her gaze with mine.

"Could you not do that?" I asked calmly.

"What?" she asked, blinking back tears.

"Apologize."

She looked at me for a second before looking away, but I took my hand and gently tilted her head back up so her eyes met mine.

"I willingly agreed to whatever happened in this room. And whatever that was, was amazing. And consensual, might I add," I continued.

She gave me a weak smile.

"You think I don't know what I signed up for when you asked me to have sex with you?"

She shrugged.

"Maybe you thought I misheard you. It did sound a little like you said, 'Do you want to have eggs with me?' Maybe I came up here expecting breakfast in the middle of the day. But no. I heard you loud and clear, and wanted to as much as you did."

She laughed at that. "You're ridiculous, you know that?" she asked, wiping away a tear.

"I know. But you know what I'm not?"

"What?"

"Upset at all by what happened."

And I really wasn't. I was surprised she was sitting here in tears apologizing for what happened between us. There was nothing, and I mean nothing, to apologize for. Sure, she had left me in bed a little dazed and confused, but life was confusing sometimes.

I had taken Kenny's advice and sat down to talk to Cleo at the barbecue afterward. She was just as shocked as Kenny to hear what had happened with Bridget. I normally wasn't one to kiss and tell like that, but they were my close friends, and they knew Bridget better than I did. I just wanted to get a grasp on the situation.

Once she sat in a stunned silence about her former boss and close friend asking me for sex, she explained to me that I probably felt so thrown off because it was my first time on that side of it. How many times had I left a woman's house in the middle of the night or the first thing the next morning? Regretfully now, too many to count. Now I knew how that felt, and yeah, it didn't feel good.

"Is that why you called me here tonight?" I asked Bridget, looking at her thoughtfully.

"Well, it wasn't for eggs." She shrugged.

It was my turn to laugh. This was the girl I knew. Dry humor. Confident. Sexy as hell.

I leaned forward and pulled her close. She buried her face in my chest and I inhaled. I breathed in her perfume that was mixed with hops from the beer. I liked that. I felt her let out a breath and sink into me more. I brushed my lips against her hair and gave her a small kiss. We sat like that for a moment in silence. This wasn't what I had expected coming here tonight. I had expected something completely different, but this was just as good.

She pulled away slightly and looked up at me. It took everything in me not to lean down and kiss her, but I didn't think that was what she wanted. I wondered if she would never want that again. The thought of being intertwined with her being a one-time thing formed a lump in my throat.

"Thank you," she said quietly.

"For what?"

"Not being an asshole."

"You thank people for that nowadays?"

She laughed.

"Look, if you never need me for that again"—my eyes trailed to the bed—"I'd be up for it."

"Oh, my God," she said, her voice an octave higher than before.

"I mean it. Or anything else… A date even."

She pulled out of my arms and eyed me in shock. I fought back a smile and shrugged casually. I meant it. I wanted to take her on a date, and that was rare for me.

"A date? With you?"

"I wouldn't mind that one bit."

She furrowed her brow as if she didn't believe me. I had told her I was not looking to settle down, and now I was sitting here asking her on a date. I was probably giving her whiplash.

"I'm serious though, date aside. If you ever need me, just call."

She nodded and gave me the smile that had come to be my favorite of hers. Her lips curled up on one side and she scrunched her nose slightly. *Perfect*, I thought.

"I better get back to the bar," she said, eyeing the door of the loft.

"Shoot, I better get back home." I looked at the clock on my phone. It was nearly midnight. Shit. I suddenly remembered I had to prep for a big meeting tomorrow.

"Everything okay?" she asked curiously.

"Yeah, work stuff."

Big work stuff. I had an early morning meeting that, if I handled it right, would surely piss my parents off. Maybe enough so that they would ignore me completely, at least for a little while. Since my dad had gotten into my mom's head about me moving home and working for him again, she hadn't left me alone. Calls. Texts. Emails. All in that "But I'm your mom" guilt-tripping tone. I couldn't handle it anymore.

That was why when I got presented with this meeting with a couple of my parents' lifelong friends and clients, I knew I had to take it. They said they were looking for someone a little younger who was up with the times in the finance world. Obviously, they hadn't told my parents about looking for someone else yet, especially that someone being me. Oh, how I would love to see the look on their faces if I did win over these clients/friends.

Usually, I was not one to do this, but my father had never once shown he cared about me in any other way than an employee. I didn't really owe him anything. Plus, if essentially stealing his clients to help them with their investments brought them more money, then it wasn't a moral issue for me. I was helping someone succeed. At least that was what I kept telling myself.

The real challenge of this was that they had a lot of overseas investments, and I needed to dissect the files they had sent me for the fifth time. I wanted to seem on my game, and as much as I'd like to stay up here with a beautiful girl, I had work to do. And so did she. That was why I liked her. She was more than a beautiful girl. She was a boss. A business owner. A success.

"Well, good luck with your work stuff," she said with air quotations.

I laughed. I hadn't meant to sound so conspicuous.

"Sorry, I just have a big meeting in the morning. So big, I might need to relieve some stress." I winked at her.

"Oh, my God." She slugged me in the arm and glared at me playfully.

"Ouch." I dramatically rubbed my arm.

"I hate you," she said.

"You love me." I took her hands and pulled her from the couch to stand.

"You wish," she whispered, suddenly realizing how close we were.

"Maybe, I do." I couldn't help it. Her green eyes looked lighter today and they were looking up at me, so I leaned in and gently kissed her. I felt her exhale into me, as if the stress of the day was melting away. I could be this for her. Her stress relief. But only if she wanted.

I pulled away slowly. Her eyes were still closed and her mouth was formed into a small smile. I brushed my thumb against her lips softly.

"I'll let you get back to it, boss." I saluted her before heading to the door. I glanced back at her before opening it and heading downstairs. She just stood there with her arms crossed, shaking her head at me slowly with an amused expression.

I only hoped it wouldn't be my last time up here with her, doing everything or nothing. It didn't matter, so long as she was there. I might not be able to slay real dragons, but whatever she was going through I wanted to be there for her.

Chapter 13

Bridget

I watched as Justin practically sauntered out the door of the loft. He not only oozed charm, but he had been really understanding about the whole sex thing. He probably came up here expecting another lay, but instead I word vomited all over him. He didn't seem to mind. Instead, he listened. Like *really* listened. Maybe I had him all wrong. Maybe he really was a good guy. And did he just ask me on a date? I shook my head as I tried to process everything.

I needed to talk to someone. It had been so long since I was mixed up emotionally with someone else. I needed girl talk. I walked to the door of the loft and peeked down the stairs. The bar was busy, but my staff was handling it well. I could make a quick call and then head back down.

I slid my phone from the back pocket of my jeans and scrolled until I found Cleo's name. I hit the call button, and hoped it wasn't too late to call.

"Hello?" she picked up groggily. I immediately felt bad.

"Hi, Cleo. Sorry it's so late."

"Bridg? Is everything okay?" She sounded more awake now, worry in her voice.

"Yeah, yeah. Everything is fine. Sorry to scare you."

"What's up?"

"Well, Justin just left, and…"

"You need a little late-night girl talk," she finished my thought.

"Yeah. Basically."

She let out a little laugh. "I feel like I'm everyone's therapist lately."

"What do you mean?"

"I just had a heart-to-heart with your man Justin the other night."

"Wait, really?" This was news to me.

"Mhmm."

I paused, not wanting to seem too eager.

"So, what did you talk about?" I asked nonchalantly.

"Well, I know you had sex."

"Cleo!" I squealed, raising my voice in embarrassment.

Yes, Cleo was my friend, but we had never really talked about relationships or sex. When she had worked here, my life was the bar. There wasn't time for anything else.

"Don't be mad at him. He was just trying to paint me the whole picture, and he honestly looked like a lost puppy. I had to help him."

"Great," I mumbled.

"Not like that. He didn't go into detail, but he did say you asked for nookie in the middle of the day. I have to say I was surprised—in a good way. Good for you for speaking up and getting some. Women have needs, too."

"Oh, my God, Cleo."

"What? It's true."

"Well, what else did he say?"

"He said he was confused. I think you just took him off guard, and then he said you left really abruptly."

I sighed. "I know, I know. I just didn't know what to do. It's not like I regretted it…at all. I think I just got caught up in the drama of my life and needed an escape. After we finished, I just thought it would be better to leave before it got any more complicated."

"Well, did it get any less complicated tonight?"

"I think it got more complicated."

"Oh."

"We didn't have sex again. I actually apologized because I felt like I had used him, which I kind of did."

"Well, then what happened?"

"He kind of maybe asked me on a date."

Cleo squealed on the other line, piercing my eardrum.

I heard Kenny mumble next to her, half asleep.

"Justin asked Bridget on a date," she said excitedly to him.

"About time. I'm going back to bed, babe," he mumbled.

"So, what did you say?" she asked, trying to keep her voice down.

"I didn't say anything."

"What? Why?"

"I don't know. I'm not really looking for a relationship. I didn't think he was either."

"Oh, my God, Bridget. It's not like he asked you to marry him."

I nodded. Maybe she was right. I was getting way too ahead of myself.

"Yeah, I know."

"You deserve to be wined and dined. Justin is a good guy. Plus, he's hot," she whispered that last part.

"Okay, okay. I'll think about it. Thanks, Cleo."

"Anytime. Well, not *anytime*. You know it's past midnight, right?"

I let out a laugh.

"I'll try to keep my girl troubles during business hours. Get back to bed. Bye."

I hung up and already felt a lot better. I was complicating things before they even started. Justin kept proving that he was different than I expected, in a good way. I already knew he was good in bed. I couldn't stop thinking about it, honestly. A date could be fun. I'd text him tomorrow.

With a smile on my face, I headed back downstairs to the bar. Andy gave me a curious look, but I just mouthed "thank you" as I passed by. The bar was emptying out a little as we approached closing time. I noticed the guy at the bar had cashed out and had left a measly tip behind. Clearly, flirting with him and then leaving with another guy had left a bad taste in his mouth. I rolled my eyes as I took the cash and added it to the tip jar behind the bar top.

The door of the bar swung open and a man walked in. He looked familiar. I watched as he made his way to the bar, trying to place him. He was wearing a suit. Greasy, slicked back hair. Nice watch. It was the guy who had been here with Cara. The one who seemed to be staking out the place. I thankfully hadn't seen him in a while, but now he was here, and I had a sinking feeling in my stomach.

"Hello, what can I get you?" I asked, mustering a smile as he sat down at the bar.

"Whiskey. Top shelf. One ice cube."

"Coming right up." I turned my back to make his drink, but I could feel him eyeing me and the bar. I didn't like it.

I handed him his drink. "I've seen you before, haven't I?" I asked casually.

"Have you?" he asked with a shrug.

He took a sip of whiskey and set his glass down. He looked at me and drummed his fingers on the countertop. What was he playing at?

"I'm Lenin," he finally said, holding out his hand.

"Bridget. I own the place." I held out my hand and firmly shook his. I hoped it was firm enough to let him know I wasn't intimidated by him.

"I know."

I looked at him curiously.

"I know your sister, Cara. You see, I'm actually into lending."

I swallowed hard. This didn't sound good.

"Is that so?" I asked, tossing a bar towel over my shoulder and leaning against the countertop. I didn't want him to see the nerves bubbling up inside of me.

"Yeah. I lent your sister ten grand. She said she was good for it, but I haven't seen a penny. I haven't seen your sister either."

My mind raced with reasons why Cara needed that much money and why she had gone to this guy to borrow it from. My sister had made some bad decisions, but this just seemed reckless. I could tell the guy was bad news just by looking at him.

"I haven't seen her either," I lied.

He crossed his arms and looked at me unconvinced.

"My sister comes and goes as she pleases. I never know where she is or what she does. She could be in another country for all I know. We aren't always on the best of terms," I continued.

"Well, I don't really need her anyway." An evil smile crossed his lips.

"Oh?" I asked.

Lenin leaned in and put his elbows on the table, looking at me with a twisted amusement that made me shudder.

"You see, your sister used you as a cosigner for the loan…"

"What? That's not possible. I've never met you in my life, and there's no way in hell I would ever agree to that," I said, my voice rising.

"It is, actually. I have the paperwork right here." He swung a briefcase onto the counter, causing a loud bang to ring out. A few customers looked over curiously. I smiled at them to reassure them that everything was okay, when in fact it was not.

Lenin clicked open the briefcase and pulled out a loan contract. I skimmed over it quickly and my eyes landed on the bottom of the page. My signature was clear as day underneath Cara's. I sucked in a breath. How could that be?

"I never signed this."

"It's notarized, sweetheart." Lenin tapped the paper as if he begged to differ.

"Bullshit," I said sharply.

"Look, it's all here on paper. He tucked the paper back in his briefcase and gently closed it."

"If your sister can't come up with the money, you'll have to."

"No. I don't have that kind of money."

"You have ten days," Lenin continued, as if he couldn't hear my protests. He picked up his briefcase and looked around the bar another time. Now I knew he was staking out the place because it might end up being his at the end of this. I couldn't bear the thought. I watched him helplessly as he strolled out the door.

I pushed my way through the kitchen doors and rushed out to the back alley into the cool night air. I sucked in several deep breaths and put my hand on the wall to support me. I felt like I was going to collapse. How did I get into this mess? How could Cara do this to me?

I snatched my phone from my back pocket and quickly scrolled through my contacts until I landed on her name. I hit the call button and was immediately met with her voicemail. I tried again. Same thing. Her phone was off. I grasped it tightly as my mind raced.

"Fuck!" I shouted up at the sky.

I kicked the asphalt before falling to sit on a curb. I dropped my face in my hands and fought back the tears that were threatening to fall. I felt completely helpless. None of this made sense, but then again it was Cara. It kind of made perfect sense. She was in another one of her messes, but this was the biggest one yet. I needed to find her.

I sat there and debated calling my dad, but it was late. It was way past his bedtime, and I didn't want to put this mess on him. He needed to stay healthy, and that meant being blissfully unaware. I even debated calling my mom, who I hadn't seen or talked to in a while. Maybe she had heard from Cara, or knew where she might be. I didn't know if I wanted to go down that road, though.

I loved my mom, but I didn't like her most of the time. She and my father had divorced a while back. It was amicable, but I knew he would never love another woman the way he loved her. And he didn't. He never remarried or even entertained the idea. If he couldn't have her, he was content with being alone. It broke my heart, but I knew they were happier apart.

When he got sick, I thought my mom would at least come back to check on him or offer to take care of him. They had shared twenty years together, after all. But no, she was off living her life with her new husband and his kids. My father's health and well-being landed solely on me.

Now *all* of this was landing on me. I didn't have ten thousand dollars lying around to get out of this mess, and if I couldn't come up with it, then I would most likely lose the bar. The thought made me burst into tears. All of my father's hard work that he had put into the place would be gone. My dream of running the place would be stripped away from me. All of this would be lost at the hands of my sister and this dirty loan shark. I could not let that happen, but how could I stop it?

Chapter 14

Justin

I tried to hide the smile that was threatening to cross my lips as I watched my new client sign the paperwork in front of him. Instead of focusing on his pen gliding across the paper, I took a sip of coffee and looked around the coffee shop. Cleo was behind the counter, boxing up some almond croissants. She caught my eye and gave me a questioning look, followed by a thumbs up or a thumbs down.

I gave her a quick thumbs up and she clapped her hands together. I decided to have my morning meeting at Cleo's bakery. It was the perfect setting. Not too uptight, and with decadent pastries to start the morning. My clients loved it as soon as they bit into their freshly fried cinnamon cronuts. See, Dad? You don't need a fancy office to sign big clients or make big deals. I smiled to myself.

"Well, I think that about covers it," Mr. Robinson said, sliding over the paperwork.

I looked it over carefully to make sure all lines were signed and initialed.

"Looks good to me. I look forward to working together." I held out my hand and shook his hand and then his wife's.

"I do hope there will be no hard feelings with your father," Mrs. Robinson said worriedly.

"Nah." I waved her away, even though I knew there would be nothing but hard feelings.

"It's just we aren't getting any younger, but we need to make sure our investments are with the times. We've seen your portfolio. You're the right man for the job," said Mr. Robinson.

"You're in good hands," I assured him with a solitaire nod.

"Well, we have a plane to catch." Mr. Robinson stood from his seat. "You'll get my copies emailed to my secretary?"

"Yes, of course. I'll have that over to you by the end of the day. Where are you two off to?"

"Bora Bora," Mrs. Robinson said, leaning in to her husband dreamily.

"Ahh."

"Have you been?" she asked.

"I can't say that I have. I hope to one day."

"Oh, you must. It's the perfect romantic destination. Do you have a special lady you can take?"

Bridget's face flashed in my mind briefly. I smiled, but shook my head. *Slow down, Justin.*

"Not at the moment," I said.

"A handsome guy like you? I find that hard to believe."

"Okay, honey. Let's go. We don't want to miss our flight." Mr. Robinson patted me on the shoulder and led his wife out the door of the bakery. When they were out of sight, I pumped my fist into the air. I had just landed the biggest client on my roster, and stolen them out from under my father. It felt good.

"That looked like it went well," said Cleo as she walked up behind me.

"It did. Maybe this is my new lucky spot." I looked around the bakery.

"I'd be honored, especially after the tip they left me. Who are they again?" she asked.

"Big wigs in the textile industry."

"Well, congrats. Maybe you can celebrate tonight. I heard you asked Bridget out." She wiggled her eyebrows at me.

How did she know that already? I had barely asked her out late last night. They must have talked, and it seemed like the conversation had weighed heavily in my favor.

"Maybe I did, but I can't tonight. I'm heading home to Boston. My mom keeps begging me to."

"Well, safe travels and congratulations." Cleo gave my arm a squeeze and walked back behind the counter to help a customer.

I gathered up my briefcase and headed home to pack an overnight bag. I quickly packed the essentials and headed down to the parking garage. I was looking forward to a nice, long drive. My parents had no idea I was coming, but I figured I could surprise them. Maybe the surprise would soften the blow of me taking one of my father's most prominent clients.

The four-hour drive went by quickly. I had the windows down and my favorite band playing through the speakers. Soon enough, I was pulling up the long, tree-lined drive to my parents' house. I noticed quite a few cars in the driveway. They must have company.

I put the car into park and walked up the steps to the wraparound porch. I heard soft music coming from the backyard. I rang the doorbell and waited a minute. When no one came, I knocked before jiggling the door handle. It was open. I stepped inside the grand foyer and followed the music.

In the backyard, a long table was set up with fresh flowers and silver trays of food in the center. At the head of the table sat my father and the other end sat my mother. In between them, sat about twenty people enjoying brunch and chattering away. Maybe I should have told them I was coming. But then again, my mother had been practically begging me for weeks.

I stepped outside and my mom glanced up suddenly. The table fell silent and I gave her a sheepish wave.

"Justin?" she said, looking at me confused. "What are you doing here?"

"Surprise." I shrugged.

She glanced at my father before rising from her seat. She gave me a hug and a kiss on each cheek. She was clearly in entertainer mode, and keeping it very professional, even though I was her son and she hadn't seen me in months.

"I guess I should have called," I whispered.

"When do you ever do what you should?" my father commented as he approached.

"Hey, Dad."

"Now is not really a good time, son."

"Allen…" my mom said softly.

He shot her a stern look. She put her hand on my back and led me back toward the door.

"I'm sorry, honey. Your father is right. It's really not the best time. Why don't you come back after?"

"You're serious?" I asked, not quite believing she was ushering me out.

"We just weren't expecting you, sweetie. As you can see, we have company." She looked outside and gave her guests a nervous smile as if I was a ticking time bomb.

"You've literally been begging me to come home. Now, here I am and you're sending me away?"

"Please, Justin. You know I'm happy to see you. Just come back later."

"Sheri. Your food is getting cold," my father called. He was back at the head of the table and looked annoyed.

I couldn't believe this. They were sending me away like I was the black sheep of the family or something. After guilt-tripping me into coming home all these weeks, now my mother is asking me to leave. I felt my face flush with anger, but I swallowed and tried to keep my cool. I took a deep breath and snatched the papers peeking out of my bag. It was the paperwork from this morning's meeting. I shoved it at her, which caught her off guard.

"Here. I thought you'd want to look at this before it went public."

She looked down at the papers, confused.

"I'm not coming back later, Mother. I forgot you don't actually care about me."

I left my mother standing on the patio, clutching the papers and looking after me sadly. I didn't bother to say goodbye to my father, who was apologizing to his guests. For what? His son coming home to surprise his parents? I hadn't even been there for five minutes and I was getting back into my car to head back to Boston. I slammed the door shut and peeled out of the driveway.

I thought after some time on the road, I would cool off, but I was still seething halfway through the drive. I decided to stop in Connecticut. Maybe a night in a different city would be good for me to get my mind off everything. I pulled into a casino off the freeway. I left my car with the valet and grabbed my overnight bag from the front seat.

After checking in at the front desk, I rode the elevator up the penthouse suite. It was way too big for just me, but I thought, what the hell? Maybe I'd bring someone up with me tonight. I tossed my bag in the bedroom and collapsed onto the bed. Maybe it was the drive or the family drama, but I was exhausted. I closed my eyes and fell asleep.

I woke up a few hours later. I was starving. I hopped in the shower for a quick rinse before changing into jeans and a T-shirt. I rode the elevator down and walked into one of the restaurant bars. It was an American grill-type place with a large bar in the center.

I took a seat at the bar and leaned back in the barstool. I felt my phone buzz in my pocket. I pulled it out and saw I had five missed calls from my mother. I listened to one of her voicemails.

"Justin, honey. I'm sorry how we left things today. Please come back. We are all done with our luncheon."

I rolled my eyes as I hit delete and played the next message.

"Justin, your father just looked over the paperwork. How could you do this to him?"

Delete.

"Justin, I know we don't always see eye to eye, but you can't take it out on your father's business. It's not right."

Delete.

I sighed as I tossed my phone on the bar top. I looked up to see a pretty bartender standing in front of me. She had short blonde hair that sat just below her ears and pink pouty lips that were pursed as she looked at me thoughtfully.

"You look like you can use a drink," she said.

"You have no idea. I'll have a—"

"Wait. Don't tell me," she interrupted.

I looked at her and raised an eyebrow.

"Whiskey on the rocks."

"How did you…"

"It's a gift." She winked and walked away to grab a glass and a top shelf whiskey.

I watched her for a moment, my eyes landing on the short skirt that left little to the imagination. Maybe she'd be the one coming up to my room later tonight.

She walked back holding a tumbler with a generous pour of deep amber liquid.

"I made it a double for you." She slid it over.

"You're good," I smiled at her. Most men I knew drank either whiskey or beer, so it really wasn't that impressive, but I figured I'd stroke her ego.

"I know." She leaned over the counter and placed her chin in her hands, looking up at me through her lashes. "So, what's got you down?"

I took a sip of whiskey.

"I'm not really in the mood to talk about it."

"I'm fine with not talking." She bit her lip as she looked at mine.

"Good to know."

I took a generous sip of whiskey and then another, finishing the glass. She pulled a bottle from behind the counter and poured me another. A customer sat at the other end of the bar, getting her attention. She gave a little sigh of frustration before looking back at me.

"Don't go anywhere. By the way, I'm off in an hour."

I watched as she walked away. I considered the possibility of spending more time with her. She was pretty. There was no doubt about that, but she didn't have an Irish accent that melted over my ears. I thought better of it and finished my drink. I left cash on the bar top and slipped out of the restaurant.

Back up in my room, I ordered a ribeye steak and a baked potato from room service. I plopped down on the couch and ate my dinner while watching bad reality TV. It wasn't the night I had expected, but I was content.

Chapter 15

Bridget

After last night's encounter with Lenin at the bar, I had to find Cara. I spent most of the day trying to find her. I went to all her usual spots, or at least the ones she frequented before she ran off to Ireland. God, I hoped she wasn't in Ireland, leaving me with this mess. I was still seething that she had got me into this. I knew if I did find her, I would have to keep a level head or else she'd run. I didn't know if I could talk rationally or calmly, but I'd have to try. First, I would have to find her.

I tried her old favorite bar. Not Murphy's, of course. She had a resentment toward the bar. I assumed it was envy because Dad had let me in on it. I had earned my place though. If she would have kept her head on straight, she could have earned her place too in whatever she wanted in life. The bar was seedy and everything my bar was not. The owner told me he hadn't seen Cara, and that she had a tab that was long and overdue. Of course, she did.

I tried the laundromat where the owner would sometimes let her crash. When I walked in and glanced at the row of chairs where my sister had most likely slept, I felt a little sadness. How did she get here? Unfortunately, the owner wasn't there. The attendant let me know he was out of town. I pulled out my phone and showed the attendant Cara's photo, but it didn't register with him.

As much as I didn't want to worry my dad, maybe I could casually get something out of him. I pulled into the driveway and sat back against the seat, taking in the view of the front yard. Cara and I used to play on the small front lawn. We'd drag our dollhouse out and traipse our dolls through the grass and my mother's rose bushes, much to her dismay. Things were so simple back then. Mom and Dad were together. Cara and I were best friends. Everything changed in high school when she began running with the wrong crowd, and clearly kept running with it.

There was a rap on my window, startling me slightly. I looked up and saw my dad looking down at me with a questioning smile. I rolled down my window.

"Hi, Dad."

"Are you coming inside or not?"

"Yes, of course. Sorry, just lost in a memory."

I rolled the window up and got out of the car, embracing my dad in a bear hug. I didn't know how much I needed him until this moment. I fought back tears as I pulled away. I hoped he didn't notice.

"What are you doing here, honey?" he asked.

"I just thought I'd pop in and check on you."

"Well, I'm happy to see you, but I'm actually on my way out."

"Out?"

"Frank wrangled me into a game of pickleball. What hell is pickleball?" he asked, scrunching his eyebrows.

I laughed. "It's like tennis, I think. And are you sure that's a good idea, Dad?"

"The doctor said some light activity would be good for me. I can't be holed up in this house forever."

I nodded, trying to push down my worry. My dad had been healthy for a while, slowly gaining his strength back. Maybe it was time for him to start living again.

"I'll be fine, Bridg," he said, as if reading my mind.

I gave him another hug and opened the door of my car, sliding into the driver's seat. My worry had almost made me forget why I was here.

"Oh, Dad. Have you seen Cara?" I asked as nonchalantly as possible.

"You know I can't keep up with her," he replied with a sigh.

"Okay." I bit my lip.

"Is everything okay? She's not in trouble, is she?"

"No, no. A friend stopped by the bar looking for her last night."

"Mhmm." He seemed unconvinced.

Before I let my cards show, I gave him a little wave and shut the car door. I had one more place to try and I hoped I could find it based on memory. I drove south and turned down a few different streets, scanning them carefully. After a few wrong turns, I finally found the apartment building I had been looking for. Cara had stayed with a friend here last year. I figured it was a long shot, but I had to try.

I parked and waited for someone to exit the building so I could slip inside. After ten minutes, a guy delivering pizza was buzzed up. I followed him inside. I climbed the dimly lit stairs to the third floor and walked down the hallway. It was apartment six. I raised my hand to knock, but was met with a yellow paper stuck to the door, an eviction notice. I tried knocking anyway, but no one answered. They were probably long gone.

Frustration washed over me as I let out a quiet moan. I slid down the door and sat on the floor, letting the tears fall. I sat there a few minutes and then it was time to try my last resort. I pulled my phone from my purse and dialed.

"Hello?" my mom's voice answered.

"Hi, Mom," I said softly.

"Bridget? Is that you?" She sounded surprised. It had been months since we had talked last.

"Yes, it's me."

"How are you, honey?"

I could hear music playing and people chattering in the background.

"I'm fine. I can barely hear you, though."

"Oh, sorry!" She giggled. I heard the music and people begin to fade.

"Can you hear me now?" she asked.

"Yes, that's better. Where are you?"

"The Bahamas! Can you believe it? Rick surprised me with a trip. You have to get out here one day!"

I rolled my eyes. Sure, when I magically find ten grand, so I don't lose the bar and then will be forever in the hole.

"Maybe one day."

"So, why'd you call, honey?"

I didn't know I needed a reason to call my own mother, but that was what our relationship had come to. I couldn't blame her for saying something that some would find offensive.

"Oh, just to see how things were. I stopped by the house today and just was sifting through memories."

"That place is still standing?" She laughed.

I ignored her jab at my childhood home. Not everyone wanted to live in a cold, minimal mansion with Rick. It pissed me off how my mom poked fun at the simple life, now that she had a brand new one. How could she be so cold about the home we grew up in? And she wondered why we didn't talk for months.

"Not the rose bushes." I bit back a smile.

I heard her huff on the other line. It worked.

"You and your sister probably killed them off all those years ago."

"Actually, Dad tended to them for years, until he got sick."

There was a pause on the other line.

"How is she, by the way?" she finally asked.

"Who?"

"Cara."

"Oh, Cara's being Cara. Have you talked to her lately?"

"No, it's been months. She calls just about as often as you do, but she usually needs something."

Well, there was no luck here. I heard the music getting louder again. My mom was heading back to the party. Clearly, our conversation wasn't interesting enough.

"Well, honey. Rick needs me for something. Oh, it's a conga line! I have to go. Good talking to you." She hung up.

I looked at my phone and shook my head. Some things never changed. I put my phone back in my purse and pulled myself to stand. It was time to call it and head home.

Once I got there, I plopped down on my couch and pulled my laptop onto my lap. I knew nothing about loan sharks. That's why I had Google. I spent the next hour scouring the web and reading horror stories about other women who had been put in a similar situation. Forgery. Threats. Bankruptcy. If I wasn't scared enough before, I was now. I didn't see a way out of this.

I closed out of the search tab and opened a new one to my bank account. I looked at my checking account. There was enough for rent and groceries. No ten grand there. I looked at my savings account. There was barely half of what Lenin had asked for.

I had nine days. Nine days to come up with an exorbitant amount of money. I shut my laptop and slid it onto the coffee table. I closed my eyes and leaned my head back on the couch. A wave of nausea hit me. I took a deep breath. Clearly, this whole mess was affecting me physically. Then I thought of something.

Sitting up straight, I grabbed my phone. I opened the calendar and counted backward, hoping I was wrong. I counted again. And again. My period was late. Not late by a few days, but nine. Nine days. Usually, my period was like clockwork. I swallowed hard and shook the thought away.

There was no way. I was sure it was just the stress of my sister being back in town and unloading her problems onto me. This shady business with Lenin was just adding to it. I sat there for a few minutes trying to convince myself, but there was only one way for sure to know. I grabbed my purse and left my apartment.

I walked down the block to the corner store. I looked around, making sure I didn't recognize anyone and that someone didn't recognize me. That someone being Justin. As much as we ran into each other, the last place I needed to see him was in the family planning aisle. I quickly scanned the shelves. There were so many options. I had never needed to take a pregnancy test before. I grabbed a box that had a few test sticks that were easy to read. I didn't want to bother with the faint lines. I wanted it to read *Pregnant* or *Not Pregnant*. I wanted it to be clear. I quickly paid at self-checkout and pushed through the doors of the store that felt like it was suffocating me.

The walk home felt like it took hours, even though it was mere minutes. I clutched the bag in my hand tightly, trying to fight off the thoughts that were running in my head. When I reached my building, I ran up the stairs to the floor of my apartment and hastily made my way inside. In the bathroom, I tore open the box and read the directions quickly. It seemed pretty simple. Pee on stick. Stick tells you your life is over, as if it wasn't already.

After sitting on the toilet, I set the test stick on the counter and set a timer on my phone.

I paced the bathroom floor. I couldn't believe that in the middle of this mess of my life, I could possibly be pregnant. I mean, it wasn't totally out of the realm of possibility. Justin hadn't worn a condom the afternoon we had sex up in the loft. It had been careless, but I was lost in the throes of stress and passion. Now, I felt like a complete idiot.

The timer on my phone went off. I snatched it up and turned it off. I stared down at the test that was face down on my counter. I took a deep breath as I waited to turn it over and have it reveal my fate. After a minute, I shakily reached out my hand and turned it over. I leaned over the counter to read what it said.

I was met with one word.

Pregnant.

Chapter 16

Justin

The morning light poured through the windows, its warmth falling on my face and pillow over my head, trying to block the light out. I squinted at the clock on the hotel nightstand: 7 a.m. I groaned. I may have had one too many whiskeys last night, along with my room service dinner. I shut my eyes tight and tried to fall back asleep.

Sleep didn't come, though. Thoughts of yesterday's encounter with my parents kept me awake. The embarrassment on their faces when I showed up on their doorstep of my childhood home. The way they practically shooed me away in front of their important friends. The way they never supported me when I wanted to build something of my own. The paperwork they had of my newest deal. The ultimate betrayal to my father. Things would never be the same after that.

I decided then that I would not go back to that house again. I knew where our relationship stood now. I was done disappointing them when all I wanted was to impress them. I had been working myself out from under my father's thumb for months now in a new city, and I was doing just fine. Better than fine. Not that I needed it, but I had access to my trust fund if I ever did. There was nothing my parents could give me anymore, and that probably killed them.

After about thirty minutes of being lost in my thoughts, I realized sleep wasn't going to happen again. I pushed the covers off me and groggily made my way to the bathroom to wash up a little. I splashed my face with water to wake up and brushed my teeth. I packed what little I brought in my overnight bag and rode the elevator down to the lobby. I needed food and a coffee.

I walked in the same bar and restaurant from last night. It was practically empty. Everyone who had gambled the night before was probably sleeping off their hangovers or losses. The hostess greeted me and sat me in a booth by the entrance.

"Your server will be right with you," she said as she handed me a menu.

"Thank you."

I began looking over the menu of basic breakfast necessities.

"Where did you run off to last night?" a voice broke my concentration.

I looked up. It was the bartender from last night. She was leaning against the table with a pen and a pad of paper, ready to take my order. I glanced at her and the glint of her nametag caught my eye: Brit.

"Oh, um. Hi. Working again?" I asked, glancing around the bar.

"Always."

I nodded sheepishly. I felt bad for leaving without saying goodbye last night. She was attractive and part of me had wanted to spend time with her after work. I could have used a little stress relief. Oh, God, I was starting to sound like Bridget.

Bridget. She was the reason I left the bar last night. It wasn't like we were in a relationship or anything, but she was all I could think about sitting there while this woman had basically offered herself up.

"Well?" Brit's voice broke through my thoughts.

"Hmm?"

"Where did you disappear to last night?"

"Oh, I had a long day."

"I could have helped you with that."

"I was tempted, but I needed to crash. Sorry."

"You can make it up to me tonight. I'm off for the evening." She leaned in even more. I could smell her perfume. Vanilla.

"I'm actually heading back to Boston this morning."

Brit gave a single nod, one that gave a hint of disappointment. She stood up straight.

"Well, what can I get you to eat then?" she asked, tapping her pen against the table. She was back to business now.

"The hash and eggs, please. And a coffee. Black. Thank you." I handed her the menu.

She took it from me rather quickly and made her way back to the kitchen.

I could have stayed. I didn't have to rush back to Boston. I had no meetings scheduled. Part of me wanted to waste the afternoon away with a beautiful blonde. Maybe throw some money away on blackjack. Enjoy a beautiful woman's company back in my room. I could certainly blow off some steam. Yet, the bigger part of me wanted to go back to Boston. It was my home now. I had grown to love the city. It was just another thing that my parents were wrong about. I wondered if it was Boston, or who was there that I longed for.

Brit brought me my coffee. I inhaled the smell before taking a sip. It instantly started to make me feel better after my solo night with whiskey. Soon, my breakfast arrived and I scarfed it down. I left some cash on the table with a generous tip before grabbing my bag and heading out of the restaurant. Another Irish goodbye.

Outside, the morning air was crisp and a world's difference from the recycled and smoky air of the casino. I took a deep breath and searched for the valet ticket in my wallet. After a minute, the valet pulled up in my car.

"Nice car, man. I've always wanted to drive one of these," said the valet. He was young. Maybe nineteen.

145

I flashed him a smile and climbed inside, tossing my bag in the backseat. I decided to put the top down on my convertible. Fresh air would do me good. I was happy I had broken it up with my impromptu stay in Connecticut. Now I just had about an hour and a half before I was home. I played some classic rock and whizzed among the cars on the interstate. I didn't know if it was the wind in my hair, or mentally cutting ties with my parents, but I felt free.

Soon, I was pulling into the parking garage of my condo. I grabbed my overnight bag and tossed it over my shoulder. I greeted the doorman happily and rode the elevator up to the top floor. I opened the door to my place and took in my surroundings. The floor-to-ceiling windows yielded unobstructed views of the city. I felt appreciative. I had made this happen for myself. I realized the validation I had been seeking from my parents had been here all along. This penthouse. This new city. My own business. I didn't need to keep searching for a pat on the back.

I took a deep breath of gratitude as I tossed my bag on the floor. I walked to my bedroom and looked around. I felt newly energized. I rocked on my heels, trying to think of something to do with this good mood. The day was mine. I had nothing scheduled, since I was supposed to be with my parents in New York.

I could call Kenny, but decided not to. The only person I really wanted to see was probably behind the bar at an Irish pub. I smiled at the thought of Bridget.

I couldn't see her like this, though. I walked to the bathroom and turned on the shower. Once the water was hot and the room was steamy, I peeled off my clothes and stepped inside. It felt good to wash off yesterday. After a long shower, I dried off and got dressed. Jeans and a black tee. The usual.

On the drive over to Murphy's, I stopped at a small market and picked up some tulips. I didn't know what made me do it. I hadn't bought flowers for a woman in a long time, if ever. It felt like a big deal. As I waited in line to check out, I texted Kenny: *I just bought flowers.*

Kenny: *I'm sure your mom will love that. But why are you telling me?*

Me: *I'm not in New York.*

Kenny: *What? I thought you were at your parents.*

Me: *I came back home. Long story.*

I saw the three dots on the screen, as if Kenny was processing.

Kenny: *Wait. So who are the flowers for?*

Me: *Bridget.*

Kenny: *Holy shit.*

Me: *I know.*

Kenny: *This is big.*

Me: *I know. What am I doing?*

Kenny: *You're crushing on a girl like a highschooler.*

Me: *Fuck.*

Kenny: *Haha. Bridg is a good one. I like this for you.*

Me: *Thanks, man.*

Kenny: *Let me know how it goes.*

I smiled and slid my phone in my pocket. I handed the cashier the flowers. She quickly rang me up and I headed back out to my car. I felt nervous, which wasn't really anything new around Bridget. Around other women, I was always confident. With Bridget, I was self-aware. She wasn't like the women I was used to.

She was a boss. Literally. She worked her ass off at the bar she owned, and had so much pride in it. It was a different career choice than mine, but didn't make it any less impressive. In fact, I was probably more impressed than anything I had built. My father would probably look down on it, but I wasn't my father and his opinion no longer mattered.

Speaking of fathers, Bridget cared about hers. A lot. When I had run into her at the grocery store and she had told me how she took care of him, I realized how special she was. I was almost envious of the relationship she shared with her father, and how much she loved him. I had never experienced that, not even as a kid.

Kenny was right. She was a good one.

I parked out front of the bar. It was early in the day and I wondered if she was even here. They wouldn't be opening for a few hours. I grabbed the flowers from the front seat and clutched them tightly as I walked up to the door. I took a deep breath and pushed it. It swung open and I walked into the dim lighting of the bar.

"We're closed," Andy called out from behind the bar.

"Hey, man."

Andy's eyes landed on me and he gave a little wave. "Oh hey, Justin. What's up?"

"Uh, just came to see Bridget. Is she around?" I asked nervously.

"She's in the office."

His eyes landed on the flowers in my hand, and I clutched them even tighter. He smiled at me knowingly and nodded to the right of the bar to a closed door.

"Thanks."

I knocked softly on the door and waited. There was no reply. I knocked again, a little harder this time. There was still no reply. I twisted the door handle and opened it slightly, poking my head inside.

I saw Bridget at her desk, slumped over with her hands in her hair. She looked up suddenly and saw me. Her eyes were red and swollen. She quickly sat up and tried brushing the tears away.

"Justin. What are you—"

I swiftly came through the door and closed it behind me. I rushed toward her, tossing the tulips on a chair. I came around the desk and knelt on the floor, pulling her into my lap. She felt rigid for a moment, and then she practically crumbled in my arms.

"Bridget, baby. What is going on?" I asked worriedly.

She began sobbing in my arms. I felt her shaking as her tears fell on my chest, dampening my shirt. I held her tightly, slightly rocking her. She didn't say anything. She just cried. I hated seeing her like this. My concern shifted to anger as I wondered who had done this to her. I wasn't a fighter, or remotely violent, but I suddenly wanted to destroy whoever made her cry.

Chapter 17

Bridget

The last thing I expected was for Justin to walk through the door when I was at my worst. I didn't realize how much I needed someone until now. Not someone. Him. My sobs only got worse as he pulled me to him. As he stroked my hair, I sank even further into his arms. I had never broken down like this in front of someone. Normally, I would feel embarrassed for not holding it together, but this felt good. I was falling apart, and I didn't care if he knew it. I felt safe as I melted into the rise and fall of his chest.

He didn't say anything, and I didn't need him to. I just needed him to hold me. It had been so long since someone had held me like this or taken care of me. It felt so damn good. I had always been taking care of everyone and everything else together. My father. My sister. The bar. I didn't realize how much of a toll it had taken on me.

I always put on this front that I was strong and could handle anything. So much so, that I actually started to believe it. It was my way of making it through. But now, with everything crashing around me, my strength—real or not—was depleting.

And on top of everything I was pregnant with this man's baby. I wished I would have blurted it out in that moment. Told him the truth. Told him everything. I didn't, though. I couldn't afford for him to run away when he was single-handedly keeping me together. Instead, I stayed silent. We stayed quiet for a while. It was comfortable. That silence drowned everything else out.

After my tears had seemed to run out, I slowly pulled away and looked up at him. He looked so worried. I managed a weak smile to ease his mind slightly. He studied my face for a second and used his thumb to gently wipe away the last of my tears. He opened his mouth to say something, but I wasn't ready to answer any questions or explain the mess that was my life. This moment was too good, so before he could utter a word, I leaned up and kissed him.

He held back at first, as if he was unsure this was the right move. To reassure him, I pressed my lips harder against his, parting them slightly. I felt him relax a little, letting out a slow breath that I breathed in eagerly. I felt his tongue graze against my top lip slowly as if he was testing the waters. I let him enter my mouth and moved my tongue against his in a steady rhythm, moaning slightly at the taste of him. He tasted so good.

God, I had missed this. I had craved this. Even though my guilt had made me put an end to it before it happened again, I couldn't stop thinking about him. Us. Intertwined. And here we were again. His mouth on mine made me forget about any guilt I had once had. I suddenly pulled away and looked up at him. His eyes were intent on mine and there was a fire behind them that there was no chance of putting out. If he was game, so was I.

I readjusted myself on his lap and slid my legs on either side of him, straddling him. He lowered his hands to my hips and held me against him firmly. I could feel him already growing hard through his jeans. It was amazing how good it felt to know how badly someone wanted you. As if I wasn't turned on enough already. I gave him a sly smile and brought my mouth to his once more. Our tongues moved more rashly this time, as if we couldn't get enough of each other.

I began moving against him, his hands guiding my hips. The roughness of his jeans and his stiffness hit me in just the right spot, making me shudder at the sensation.

His hands moved from my hips, up my shirt, his fingers trailing against my bare skin. He skillfully tugged my shirt over my head and tossed it aside. Our mouths parted for a second before his was back on mine, even more hungry than before. I felt his fingertips press into the flesh of my upper and lower back as I continued grinding against him.

He moved his lips from mine, down my neck with slow, sensual kisses. He ran his tongue across my collarbone lightly as his fingertips met the clasp of my bra. He unhooked the clasp and slid the straps down my shoulders, my bra falling to the floor. He leaned back slightly, his eyes taking me in as my breasts spilled before him. I arched my back slightly, inviting him to do as he wanted. Begging him to.

He placed his hand at my lower back, supporting me as his other hand gently grabbed the hair at the nape of my neck. He pulled slightly, causing me to hitch my back even more. I sucked in a breath as I felt his against me. It felt like torture waiting. Then his tongue lapped against my nipple gently. I let out a sigh of pleasure as he took my breast into his mouth, his tongue swirling around my erect nipple.

Strong hands held me in place as he continued taking my breasts into his mouth. The sensation of his wet mouth on my nipples and his hand knotted in my hair was making me soak through my panties. I needed more. I needed it now.

"Justin," I whispered.

He untangled himself from my hair, and I brought my head back up to look at him. I was breathing heavily. My eyes must have said everything. He gave me a single nod before lifting me off him. He grabbed a blanket from my desk chair and laid it down in one swift motion before lowering me onto it.

His fingers tugged at the waistband of my leggings, pulling them down and off my legs. His eyes grazed over my black lace thong. He shifted down until his face was directly over me. Eyes met mine as he breathed against the lace, causing me to clench in anticipation. He slid his hand over me lightly and raised his eyebrows sexily.

"You're so wet."

I bit my lip as I stared back at him. He pulled my panties aside and kissed me, his eyes never leaving mine. Holy shit, this was hot. I tried to keep my eyes on his as his tongue moved against me, his finger moving in sync in and out of me. I couldn't hold his intense stare and threw my head back with a gasp.

He continued kissing me, his breath heavy as my hips quaked beneath him. He dipped a long finger into me, prying me open even more. He traced his tongue around me in purposeful circles. I was losing control. My hands grabbed the edges of the blanket, my knuckles white. I let out a loud moan as I released against his open mouth.

Soon he was hovering over me, looking toward the door nervously. It was unlocked. Anyone could come in. He put his finger to my lips. I opened my mouth and lowered it around his finger, sucking slowly. His eyes widened before shaking his head slightly.

"You're something else. You know that?" he said.

I reached down to the waistband of his jeans and undid the button. I unzipped them and shimmied them down his hips. He kicked them off and my hands were immediately at his briefs. There were still too many layers between us. I slid them off down his hips and my eyes fell to his erection that spilled out. I sucked in a breath as he kicked his briefs to the side.

He held himself above me, his muscular arms on either side of my shoulders. I parted my legs. I never needed anything more, and he knew it. He smiled down at me wickedly as he lowered himself against me. I could feel the tip of his erection against the lace of my panties. I felt myself throb with yearning. I reached down to take them off, but his hands were suddenly on mine, holding them beside my head. He gathered them together with one hand and held them in place.

His fingers ran down my stomach until they reached the edge of my panties. He slid a finger under and pulled them to the side. His eyes left mine and fell. I parted my legs even more and he sucked in a shaky breath.

I watched as he slid his erection against me. I clenched as he slowly moved against me, teasing me. I lifted my hips to meet him, to have him enter me, but he pulled back. From the look on his face, he was enjoying this. I lowered my

156

hips frustratedly. He was back against me now, his tip against my wet opening. Our eyes watched as he dipped into me slightly before pulling back out. I squirmed underneath him, but his hand held mine in place strongly.

He dipped into me again, another inch this time. I felt myself growing wetter. He pulled out slowly.

"Fuck me," I whispered.

Then his eyes were on mine. Intent. On fire.

Then he slid inside, every inch filling me. He seemed to stop breathing as he held himself inside, taking it all in. Then he began thrusting harder, slamming into me. His breath was heavy now. My hands were still held above my head. I was losing all control and I loved every second of it. He slipped with ease in and out, our flesh pounding together.

Suddenly, he let go of my hands and he lifted my hips, turning me over, with my hands and knees on the floor. He slid off my stretched out, wet panties. He ran his hands up the back of my thighs until they gripped my hips and positioned himself behind me. I closed my eyes as I braced myself.

He entered me swiftly and with ease. He continued slamming into me, his fingers digging into the flesh of my hips.

"Fuck, Bridget," he moaned. His breath was haggard as he began to slow.

I lifted myself onto my knees, never letting him leave me. I raised my arms and wrapped my hands around the back of his neck. I began swirling against him, him touching every inch of me. He moaned as his hands reached up and cupped my breasts.

I eased myself up and off him before sliding down onto him again. I grinded against him, my back to his chest, his fingers kneading my breasts. I began moving rhythmically against him. I was peaking again. I could feel him begin to throb inside of me, his grip tighter on my breasts. I let go at that moment, letting out a quiet scream as he filled me.

We both fell forward, him tumbling on top of me. He rolled off me and lay on his back, trying to catch his breath, as I did the same. After a minute, he pulled me close to him and I laid my head on his chest. I listened as his breathing began to slow.

I leaned up to look at him. God, he was beautiful. I couldn't help but grin.

"What?" he asked curiously, fighting back a smile.

I shrugged innocently.

He shook his head and let out a dramatic sigh.

"You know, one of these days you're gonna have to actually talk to me. And the irony of me being the one to suggest you talk feelings is not lost on me, I know."

I laid my head back on his chest and laughed.

Chapter 18

Justin

As Bridget lay on my chest, I realized how different it felt than last time. The sex was phenomenal. That wasn't different. I wondered if it was possibly better, if that were even possible. But no, Bridget was still here syncing her breath to mine and enjoying the silence. She wasn't rushing to get dressed and leave.

My intention in coming to see her today wasn't to ravage each other in the side office of her bar. I just wanted to see her. If my time in New York taught me anything, it was you can choose who you want to be in your life. And if my time in the casino restaurant taught me anything, it was that I only wanted Bridget.

I traced my hands up her arms as she nuzzled in closer. I still had questions for her, like why she was crying. I didn't want to pressure her though. I hoped she would tell me when she was ready. Just thinking about her sitting slumped on her desk looking so distraught brought on the familiar feeling of anger and protectiveness I had felt when I walked in here. I wanted to knock out whoever had hurt her. At the very least, I wanted to take care of her, if she'd let me.

"Why'd you come here today?" she murmured.

"I wanted to see you."

"You missed me, huh?" she chided.

"Is it totally cheesy to admit that I did?"

"Not terribly cheesy. Just the right amount."

I laughed and kissed the top of her head. "I wasn't expecting *that*," I said.

"It wasn't on my agenda either." She laughed, burying her head in my chest.

My stomach grumbled then. I realized I was hungry after the drive from Connecticut and the workout we just had here on the floor.

"You hungry?" she asked, looking up at me and raising an eyebrow.

"Famished."

"Me too."

She rolled off me and stood up to find her clothes. I propped myself up on my elbows and admired her. Her red hair fell in loose waves above her lower back. Her curves were just right. It took everything in me not to pull her back down to the blanket with me. She turned and caught me looking, but she didn't cover up. Instead, she smiled slightly as if she knew she was giving me a show.

"You better get some clothes on or there will be a round two," I said.

She slid on her lace panties, not breaking eye contact with me, which was all the more sexy. I stood up and strode toward her, putting my hands on her hips and trailing the hem of her panties.

"I mean it," I whispered in her ear.

She pressed her body against mine, and for a second I thought we might be at it again. But she stood on her tiptoes and gave me a soft kiss.

"We have to eat. And the bar opens soon," she said.

"Fiiiine." I rolled my eyes.

She laughed as she continued getting dressed. I found my clothes and pulled them on. She ran her fingers through her hair and wiped her under eyes gently.

"You look beautiful," I said.

"Thank you. You ready to head out there?"

"And face Andy who just heard everything?" I asked.

She put her face in her hands and peeked at me through her fingers. "Was I really that loud?"

"No, not at all." I winked.

She grabbed my hand and dragged me out of the office and out into the bar. They were still closed, so thankfully there were no customers whose ears had borne witness. There was Andy, however. He looked up from the bar and gave us a sly smile. He opened his mouth to say something, but Bridget held her hand up.

"Not a word or you're fired."

Andy motioned that he was zipping his lips.

Bridget led me to a corner booth and we both sat down.

"Have you tried our burgers yet?" she asked.

I shook my head.

"Andy, is Martin here yet?" she called out.

"Yeah, he just got in," said Andy.

"Can you tell him to grill up some burgers?"

"On it, boss."

"The whole boss thing is pretty sexy," I said, leaning back in the booth and admiring her.

She waved me off, but I saw her cheeks turn rosy.

Our food came out quickly, and we both scarfed it down. It was delicious with fried onions and bacon. I was impressed Bridget kept up with me. Clearly the afternoon had taken it out of both of us. After my last bite, I patted my stomach.

"Good, right?" she asked, licking her fingertip of sauce.

"Better than good."

We sat in silence for a moment, digesting everything. The burger and what transpired between us. Again. Then, I had to ask.

"So, when I came to see you earlier…" I ventured.

"Oh, it was nothing," she said quickly.

"Bridget." I narrowed my gaze.

She let out a sigh and studied my face, as if she was trying to decide if she could trust me. I reached my hand across the table and placed it on hers, giving it a squeeze. I wanted her to tell me, but only if *she* wanted to.

"I'm in a bit of a mess," she said quietly.

"What kind of mess?"

"The kind where I owe someone ten grand."

"What the hell, Bridg?" It came out of my mouth before I could stop it. I hoped it wasn't too judgmental.

"I know, I know. My sister got me into this mess though."

"Your sister?"

She nodded. "Cara. She's always been reckless. I'm used to it. I always clean up her messes and help her when I can. But this time…"

She dropped her head in her hands.

I scooched over in the booth so I was next to her and put my arm around her. "What happened?"

"She got mixed up with a really shady guy. A loan shark. His name is Lenin. I've seen him around the bar a lot lately, or outside staking the place. He finally came in the other night and told me that Cara owes him ten grand. He can't find her. I can't find her."

"Okay, but it's not your problem."

"It is when my name is on the loan."

"Why would you sign off on that?" I asked, trying to keep my voice down. Bridget seemed smarter than that.

"I didn't! Somehow, my signature is forged on the contract. He brought in the papers and everything when he came in the other night."

"Jesus, there has to be a way to fight this. A lawyer or something."

"By the time I hire a lawyer, the fees will be just as much, if not more, than he's asking for."

I nodded. She was right.

"I'm scared, Justin."

"Did he threaten you?"

"He said if I don't come up with the money, I'll lose the bar."

She started crying on my shoulder and I held her tightly. I couldn't believe her sister would do this to her. Not only had she put Bridget's livelihood in jeopardy, but she also put her in danger. Loan sharks were no joke. I was suddenly livid.

"Hey, hey, hey," I said calmly, pulling her away and looking her in the eye. "We'll find a way out of this mess."

"No, this isn't your problem. It's mine."

"When do you have to pay him?"

"In like a week," she sniffled.

165

Immediately, I wanted to offer her the money to get her out of this mess. Ten grand was no skin off my back. I wouldn't even know it was gone, but I couldn't tell her that. Hell, if ten grand meant it would keep her safe, I'd pay more. Way more. But what I knew of Bridget was she was a strong woman who prided herself on that. I didn't want to rush in and play hero if she didn't want me to. She didn't seem like the type to be the damsel in distress, despite the dream of her being saved by me from the dragon. Her independence was part of the reason I liked her so much.

Because I liked her so much, I didn't want to scare her away by overstepping. This whole thing between us, whatever it was, was new. Although I thought it had ended, it was clearly not over. This afternoon was proof of that. Something in me had started to change since I met her. There was something between us that I wanted to see through. I knew I had told her that I wasn't the settling down type, but with her it was different. With her, I wanted to try.

Straight up offering her money was out, but I could help her in other ways. I leaned my forehead against hers and wiped her tears away.

"I want to help you," I said.

"I don't know how you can," she said, shaking her head against mine.

I pulled back and took her hands in mine. She took a deep breath and looked at me as she tried to gather herself.

"Look, you might not know this about me, but I'm a financial advisor."

"Yeah…Cleo mentioned it." She shrugged cluelessly.

"I help people make money. A lot of money. I manage their investments, help them create strategies to build their income."

"I don't have any investments. This bar is my investment." Bridget looked longingly around. I knew how much it would pain her to lose it.

"That's okay. I can still help you with whatever you have. If you need proof, ask Kenny. I helped him build his wealth."

"No offense, but Kenny is a major league ball player. I'm a bar owner."

"I helped him start a small portfolio before he made it to the big leagues. We've known each other for years. You don't need much to start. Whatever you can invest, I can make it grow."

Bridget looked at me unconvinced. I had to convince her.

"Bridg. I'm good at what I do. I know it sounds like a gamble, but it's not. I've worked my ass off. Hell, I have more money than I know what to do with. I mostly went off on my own to start my own business to piss off my parents, but it took off."

Shit. I hoped that didn't sound too cocky.

Bridget raised an eyebrow at me. She was clearly not impressed by that. I didn't need her to be. I was more than okay with her not giving a damn about what was in my bank account. I liked that she wasn't turned on by wealth and status. I had dealt with far too many women who were with me for the wrong reasons. Still, I was just trying to convince her that I knew my craft, and that I could help her out of this.

"I don't know, Justin." She bit her lip nervously.

"I know it's a lot to think about. I just want to help in any way I can. If you'll let me."

"Thank you. I'll think about it."

I put my hand to her cheek and she rested her face against it, looking at me. She seemed to be a little more at ease, but I still hated to see her worry like this.

"I better get things ready for the bar to open," she said, glancing at the clock on the wall.

"Of course," I said.

I pulled my wallet out of my jeans to pay for the food, but she waved me off.

"Lunch is on me."

We stood from the booth and I felt Andy's curious eyes on us. She must have, too, because she gave me an awkward kiss on the cheek.

"Take care of yourself, okay?"

She nodded.

"I mean it. Call me if you need anything."

I gave a smirking Andy a wave as I headed out the door. I was happy I had shown up here today. If I hadn't, I would never have known the trouble she was in. I hoped she would let me help her.

Chapter 19

Bridget

I avoided Andy's gaze as I made my way behind the bar to make sure the kegs were full and ready for the night. I busied myself with polishing the glassware, while my mind was busy with thoughts of Justin. He had just left, but his impression on me was still ripe. How did my afternoon go from crying at my desk to ending up in a tangled heap on the floor? If memory served me right, he had brought flowers. Tulips, I think. I wondered how or if he knew they were my favorite.

I also wondered what they meant. Justin didn't seem like the flower type, but then again, he had proved me wrong in a lot of things. Whatever this thing between us was, was turning into something. I smiled to myself as I straightened the liquor bottles on the shelf.

"What's going on with you two?" Andy pried.

"Huh?" I asked, breaking my own thoughts.

"You and business hottie." Andy wiggled his eyebrows at me.

I couldn't help but laugh. I noticed Andy check out Justin a few times, and he was always up for girl talk. He had become a good friend of mine.

"We're just hanging out."

"Is that what you call it these days?" Andy's eyes shot to my closed office door.

"Shut up." I tossed a rag at him.

"I had to turn the music up to drown you out." He laughed.

"Oh, my God." I hid my face in my hands in embarrassment. I could feel it turning bright red.

"Hey, no judgment. In fact, I'm a little jealous. Of you, not him," he clarified.

"You should be." I winked at him.

"Ooooh," he sung, raising his eyebrows at me as he danced around the back bar.

Just then, the bar door swung open then and our first customers walked in. *Let the madness begin.* There was a playoff game tonight, so we were going to be busy.

The night went by quickly. We had our regulars, our sports fanatics, and a bachelor party. It was chaos, but the best kind. I loved a busy night at the bar. I was relieved that Lenin didn't come by again. Every shift I had been feeling anxious, looking over my shoulder to see if he was there. I wondered when I would see him again, but at least it wasn't tonight.

As I walked the last customer out and made sure they got an Uber home, I walked back into the bar and closed the door, locking it behind me. Andy turned off the music and began counting tips behind the bar. I started clearing the tables and wiping the beer stains from the wood.

I love this place, I thought as I looked around. I knew a lot of people wouldn't find as much pride in serving people drinks and cleaning up after them, but it was more than that. It was about having a place that people could call home. Our regulars were like family.

Along the walls of the place were framed photos of my father and baseball players who had visited. There were Polaroids of customers collaged along the wall too. There were so many memories in this place, even long before I stepped foot in it as a baby. The idea that it could be taken away was too much to bear.

It had felt good to open up to Justin about everything over lunch. I had been holding everything inside because I didn't want anyone to worry, but it was inevitable I would break down. I was glad it was with him. Spending the afternoon with him had made me feel better. Safe, in a way.

I couldn't believe he had offered to help me. He really was a good guy. Still, we hardly knew each other. As much as I wanted to trust him, I didn't know if I knew him well enough to accept his help. This was laughable, considering I was carrying his baby. Oh, God, the baby. My

172

stomach sank. I wanted to tell him I was pregnant, but I was already unleashing enough problems on him. Besides, I hadn't even gone to the doctor yet.

A thought popped in my head. What if he thought I got pregnant to manipulate him? Some women do that, especially to rich men. I hoped he didn't think I had done it on purpose. We had both gotten lost in the moment. We were both at fault for not using protection.

The truth was, I didn't care about his money. Material things didn't interest me. Plus, I was still lost on what his job even was. When he was talking about what he did, it all seemed so foreign to me. Another reason I didn't feel comfortable accepting his help. I barely had anything to give. I didn't understand how he could magically make my money grow.

The situation with Lenin seemed impossible, but I would have to figure out a way out of this mess on my own. It was my problem, and I would have to exhaust every possible solution to not lose the bar. If I failed, then at least I knew I had Justin as a last resort.

"Why don't you go home, boss," said Andy, handing me my half of the tips. It was a generous amount after a busy night.

"There's still a lot to do." I folded the money and tucked it in my pocket. Everything I made was going straight into my savings account. Every little bit helped, even though I was far from having enough to pay Lenin back.

"I've got it. You look tired, and I mean that in the nicest way."

I put my hand on his shoulder and gave it a squeeze. "Thanks, Andy. I don't know what I would do without you."

"I know, I know. Go get some rest." He practically shooed me away.

Rest did sound good. I hung my apron on the hook by the kitchen door and walked to my office. I opened the door, closing it behind me. I tidied up a little and noticed the tulips on my chair. He *did* bring me flowers. I picked them up and breathed them in. They were beautiful. Pink, purple, yellow. I hugged them before I headed out the door. I locked up the office and waved goodbye to Andy.

The drive home was short, and I was relieved to pull up to my brownstone. That was until I saw Cara sitting on the steps. Her red hair was pulled up into a messy bun, and she was wearing ratty sweats and a T-shirt. She had her knees pulled in, head down. She must not have heard me pull up.

I parked and clambered out of my car, slamming the door behind me.

"You have a lot of nerve to show up here," I said loudly.

She jerked her head up and looked up at me groggily. I wondered if she had been sleeping. How long had she been waiting for me here? Why hadn't she gone to the bar? Probably to avoid any run-in with Lenin.

"Hey, sis," she said meekly.

"Don't 'hey, sis' me. Do you even know the mess you've gotten me into?"

Cara's eyes grew wide with realization.

"Yep. I know everything. Lenin paid me a visit the other night. Ten grand, Cara? Really?!" I shouted.

"I'm going to pay him back."

"Not fast enough, apparently. He's coming after me now. How the hell did my name end up as a cosigner on your loan?"

Cara dropped her head in her hands and started crying. I couldn't even muster up any sympathy for her. I just stood there with my arms crossed waiting for answers.

"Well?" I asked after a minute.

"I'm so sorry, Bridget. I didn't know what to do. I thought I could pay him back and you would never be the wiser. He wouldn't give me the loan without a cosigner."

"An unwilling cosigner. How is that even legal?"

"I don't know. He's a loan shark. They do things differently." Cara's voice was shrill.

"I'm going to lose the bar, Cara. Dad's bar. How could you do this?"

Cara fell silent. She couldn't look at me. I studied her face for any remorse, and my eyes landed on a bruise on her cheek. I rushed to her side.

"Cara, what happened?" I brushed my thumb lightly over the bruise.

She winced. "It's nothing," she lied.

"Bullshit."

"Can I stay the night? Just for tonight?" she asked, her eyes watering.

I studied her for a moment. She looked so frail. So scared. I let out a sigh and gave in. The last thing I wanted to offer her was a place to stay, but seeing that she might be in danger, I had no choice.

"Just for tonight."

I stood up and searched my purse for my keys. I unlocked the door and stepped inside, Cara following behind me like a sad puppy dog. She stood in the living room awkwardly as I went to the kitchen. I grabbed an ice pack from the freezer and met her back in the living room.

"Sit," I said firmly.

I handed her the ice pack.

"Thank you." She took the ice pack and held it gently against her cheek.

I had so many questions, but I just couldn't find the strength to talk to her right now. I was so angry. I had tried to find her for days, searching for her and calling her. Now she was here, and I could barely look at her.

I turned and walked to the linen closet. I pulled down some bath towels and a blanket. I tossed them beside her without another word and headed upstairs.

I took a hot shower and wrapped a towel around me. Downstairs was quiet. I wondered if she had fallen asleep. I quietly walked to my bedroom and closed the door. I slid on a large shirt and shorts and sat down in bed. I turned on the TV for some background noise.

My mind was racing. As much as I wanted to sleep, I couldn't. I grabbed my phone and scrolled to Cleo's name. She had been my confidant when we worked together, but we didn't see each other as much anymore since she opened up her bakery. I didn't want to stress her out with my problems, especially since the last time I called her I had woken her up with boy problems.

I chewed on my lip as I continued scrolling through my contacts. I fell on Justin's name and typed out a text. I sent it before I could talk myself out of it.

Me: *Hey. Are you up?*

I watched the three dots bounce across my screen immediately.

Justin: *Is this a booty call?*

Me: *Haha. No.*

Justin: *Darn.*

Me: *I could use a distraction though.*

Justin: *I'm your guy.*

I settled into the fluffy pillows resting against my headboard.

Me: *What are you doing?*

Justin: *It's 3 AM. I'm in bed.*

Me: *Did I wake you?*

Justin: *No. I'm watching TV. Couldn't sleep.*

Me: *Same. What are you watching?*

Justin: *Schitt's Creek. Have you seen it?*

I looked up at my TV and smiled. We were watching the same thing. I scrolled through *Schitt's Creek* memes and sent him my favorite one.

Justin: *Haha. That's my favorite one.*

Me: *Mine too. Speaking of, how did you know tulips were my favorite?*

Justin: *I didn't. They just suited you.*

I could feel myself blush.

Me: *Well, thank you.*

He sent another *Schitt's Creek* meme. We spent the next hour texting about the episode we were watching. I forgot all about my sister downstairs, and finally fell asleep just after 4 a.m. with a smile on my face.

Chapter 20

Justin

I woke up to my phone vibrating with a new text message. I groaned as I groggily rolled over to my stomach. I began searching lazily for it in the sheets. I must have fallen asleep texting Bridget. It was the wee hours of the morning when she texted me in the first place. It came as a surprise to see her name on my screen. She needed a distraction and I was happy to do it.

My hand found my phone underneath my pillow. I slid it out and closed one eye as the screen lit up annoyingly bright. It was a text from Bridget. I smiled just seeing her name. I glanced at the time at the top right corner. It was nearly noon. I hadn't slept this late in a long time. With the blackout shades in my room, I was none the wiser that it was practically midday.

I sat up against my headboard and flipped the switch on the wall next to me. The motorized shades began to raise in unison, revealing the city below. Bougee, I know. I blinked a few times as my eyes adjusted to the sunlight. Then I opened the text from Bridget: *Sorry, I fell asleep on you.*

Me: *It's okay. I did too. I haven't slept this late since college.*

Bridget: *Haha. Welcome to my life. I'm practically nocturnal as a bar owner.*

Me: *How was it last night?*

Bridget: *It was packed. Playoffs. You know.*

I actually didn't. Besides watching Kenny's games, I didn't know much else outside of his team. I truthfully wasn't much of a sports guy.

Me: *Right. Did you sleep okay?*

Bridget: *Better than I have in a while, thanks to you.*

Me: *To me?*

Bridget: *We had a tiring afternoon ;)*

Me: *That we did.*

My mind was immediately back in her office, on the blanket, my hands on her, and her mouth on me. I wanted to do it again. And again. But I didn't know what we were exactly. I hoped to find out.

Me: *Maybe we could see each other outside of the bar sometime…*

Bridget: *Like a date?*

Me: *Yeah.*

I waited impatiently as the three dots bounced on my screen for about a minute.

Bridget: *I'll have to think about it.*

That wasn't the response I hoped for and now I felt foolish.

A moment later, she texted again.

Bridget: *I'm sorry. I just have a lot going on right now.*

Me: *Yeah, I understand.*

She did have a lot going on. I did understand. I just felt like the afternoon in her office meant something more. Things seemed different after that. We had just spent the whole night talking over the phone. She was the one who texted me first. Maybe I had misunderstood whatever this was.

A calendar notification popped up on the screen. Shit. I had a meeting in less than an hour.

Me: *Well, I better get up. I have a meeting soon. Talk soon?*

Bridget: *Okay.*

I rolled out of bed and headed to the bathroom. I rushed to take a quick shower and brush my teeth. I had almost forgotten about my one o'clock meeting. Never would I have thought I needed to set an alarm for so late in the day. If Bridget was going to be in my life, I might have to get used to this.

Thankfully, the meeting was at my client's office that was at a nearby high rise. I had just enough time to stop in at Dunkin for my usual coffee. I ordered an Americano and waited for the barista to call my name. Looking around, I bet Bridget would be here soon too. I wished I could stay to find out, but instead, I quickly paid and strode down the block.

My meeting went well. My client was pleased with what his investments brought in for the month. With how successful the month was, we didn't need to make any changes to his portfolio. Why fix something that's not broken?

"How is your old man, Justin? It's been a long time," he asked as I began packing up my briefcase.

"Oh, same old, same old," I said.

The truth was, I hadn't spoken to my father since I left New York last weekend. Afterward, my mom had called and left guilt-tripping voicemails I was sure he put her up to. Then he was sending me emails talking about business etiquette and how stealing clients from under him was not a good look. Of course, he didn't call me. My father didn't do well in sharing his emotions. He was much better behind a computer. He was kind of like a robot.

"Well, please tell him I said 'hello.'"

"Of course. Same time next month?"

"Yes. Will you let my secretary know on your way out?"

"Yes, sir."

After setting up an appointment for the following month, I headed back toward my place. The weather was perfect. I was glad I had decided to walk. As I strolled, my phone buzzed in my pocket. I was pleasantly surprised it was Bridget. We'd never really texted before. I wasn't sure if last night was a one-time thing.

Bridget: *How was your meeting?*
Me: *Good. Better than good.*
Bridget: *Good!*

Me: *How many times can we say good?*
Bridget: *Haha.*
Me: *How are you? Do you still need distracting?*
Bridget: *I'm better now. Thank you by the way.*
Me: *You never did tell me what happened.*
Bridget: *My sister showed up last night.*
Me: *Oh.*

Bridget: *Yeah. That was quite a surprise when I got home from the bar.*

Me: *Did you talk to her about everything?*

Bridget: *I wish. I was too tired and angry to talk. I let her crash on my couch, but she was gone when I woke up.*

Me: *Shit.*

Bridget: *Yeah. I'm worried about her. She looked roughened up.*

Me: *I'm so sorry.*

Bridget: *Me too.*

I felt bad for Bridget. It seemed like she was always taking care of everyone around her. Her dad. Her sister. I didn't know much if anything about her mom. Her big heart was what drew me to her, but I didn't like how her sister had used her like this. I wanted to offer my help again, but I figured she would come to me if she really needed me.

Bridget: *What's your favorite food?*

I read the text and laughed. She really knew how to change the subject.

Me: *Need me to distract you again?*

183

Bridget: *Yes, but I also want to know. I hardly know anything about you. What's your last name?*

Me: *Ralston. Yours?*

Bridget: *Quinn.*

Me: *What's your favorite food?*

Bridget: *Spaghetti and meatballs. Yours?*

Me: *Sushi.*

Me: *What's your favorite color?*

Bridget: *Yellow. Yours?*

Me: *Blue.*

Bridget: *What's your favorite animal?*

Me: *Elephant. Yours?*

Bridget: *Platypus.*

Me: *Seriously?*

Bridget: *Yes, they're cute!*

Me: *Haha.*

She sent a meme of a platypus. I had to admit it was pretty cute.

Me: *Fine. It's cute. You win.*

Bridget: *Ha. Favorite dessert?*

An answer immediately came to mind, but I didn't know if I could actually type it out and send it. I stood at the street corner, waiting for the light to change. Screw it. I typed a short text and hit send.

Me: *You.*

Bridget: *Justin!*

Me: *What? It's true.*

Bridget: *My face is fifty shades of red right now.*

Me: *Oops.*

Bridget: *You're something else, you know that?*

Me: *So are you.*

Over the next few days, we texted all day, every day. I felt like I was in high school again. I would text her between meetings and she would text me when she could from the bar late at night. We continued getting to know each other. The big things. The small things. The heavy. The light. Sending memes. Taking selfies. The more I learned about her, the more I liked her.

Several times during our marathon texting, I wanted to attempt asking her on a date again, but I hadn't worked up the nerve to be rejected again. It didn't have to be a big ordeal. I'd be happy just to sit in the park and talk to her again. Or grab a coffee together.

I didn't bring it up again, though. Like she said, she had a lot going on. I didn't want to complicate things. I also didn't want to rush things. Not that there was anything left to be rushed. We went straight to home base pretty quickly. Despite that, I wanted to take my time getting to know her. I wanted to do things right.

In the past, I hadn't been interested in taking the time to really get to know anyone. I was down for a good time, but that was it. No one intrigued me enough to go further than a good party and a possible lay. Later, my friends had started to settle down, but I was convinced that life was not for me. I had my business and that was all I needed. Maybe that was my father in me. He and my mom were high school sweethearts,

185

but he didn't have time for her once he became successful.

I sat at my desk that Wednesday, going over a new contract and reviewing portfolios. My phone buzzed. I quickly reached for it. I tried not to be disappointed when I saw Kenny's name on the incoming call.

"Hello?"

"Wow. Is this Justin?"

"Yeah…" I replied confused.

"I didn't know you were still alive."

"Oh haha."

"Where have you been, man?"

"I've just been busy."

"Mhmm," he replied, unconvinced.

"What?" I asked innocently.

"How is Bridget?"

I shrugged. "Oh, she's good. I think."

"You *think*? Cut the shit, man. You brought her flowers the other day!"

I forgot I had told him.

"Oh, right."

"Cleo said Bridget stopped by the bakery the other day and her phone was blowing up. She said she couldn't type fast enough, and saw your name on the screen. What's going on with you two?"

I sighed. "I don't know, Kenny…"

"You caught feelings, didn't you?" He laughed on the other line.

"Bad."

"It's about time!"

"This is new for me," I confessed.

"I know. It was for me too with Cleo."

"Okay, slow down. I'm not asking her to marry me like you did."

"Haha. Okay. But when you do, you owe me. I *did* introduce you two."

"Noted."

"Well, I gotta head into training. Just wanted to make sure my best friend wasn't dead in a ditch somewhere," he said.

"I'm alive and well. Talk to you later."

"Later."

I hung up and slid my phone on my desk. I leaned back in my chair and spun around, thinking about what Kenny said. It was way too soon to even think about dating, let alone marriage. Still, a small part of me was opening up to the idea of settling down. I laughed as I thought about one of my first conversations with Bridget, when I said I would never settle down. Now, here I was considering it and it was with her.

I really did need to thank Kenny for setting this up. I wondered if he had masterminded the whole thing, or if it was just coincidence. Either way, I began a mental list of ways to thank him.

Beer.

More beer.

New custom shoes.

Beer.

He really was a simple man.

My phone buzzed again on my desk. I spun around and grabbed it, prepared to take more shit from Kenny. I was happy to see a text from Bridget. I quickly opened it.

Bridget: *Can we talk money?*

This was not the text I was expecting, but one I gladly welcomed. I hoped she would eventually come to me for help, especially since her deadline was coming. But I knew it had to be on her own time.

Me: *Where are you?*

Bridget: *Murphy's.*

Me: *I'm on my way.*

I stood from my chair and tucked my laptop under my arm. I grabbed my keys from my entry table and jogged to the elevator, then down to the parking garage. I was ready to help get her out of this mess. I wanted to help her more than anything.

Chapter 21

Bridget

I drummed my fingers on my desk as I looked at the paper calendar laid out in front of me. I had been crossing each day off as the deadline to pay Lenin loomed ahead. Three more days. I had three more days to come up with ten thousand dollars. It was so impossible that it was almost laughable.

The bank took humor in my situation, too. Of course, they didn't know the reason I needed so much money practically overnight. But still, when I visited the bank this morning, the teller took one look at her computer and looked at me like I was crazy.

"Ms. Quinn, unfortunately you don't have enough credit to qualify for a loan at this time."

"I own a bar. Does that count for anything? It's Murphy's Pub. Do you know it?"

"I can't say I do," she said, looking at me over her glasses.

"Oh."

"Look, even if there was a possibility of you qualifying, it would take weeks for you to receive the money for a loan."

"So, you can't help me?"

"I'm sorry, but no."

I had left feeling entirely defeated. I headed to Murphy's afterward. I let myself in and locked the door behind me. I had the desire to make myself a drink. I pulled whiskey from the top shelf and grabbed a glass. Before I began to pour, I stopped myself.

The baby.

What was I doing? In everything, I had almost forgotten about being pregnant. I had finally gone to the doctor yesterday to confirm what the test had said. I was, in fact, pregnant. My eyes watered at the thought. What was I going to do? I couldn't tell Justin. I would figure it out. I had always taken care of myself. Now was no different.

First things first was dealing with Lenin, though. I looked around the bar. I had to figure out something. All my money was tied up here. I thought maybe I could sell some equipment off or maybe some of the autographed photos we had behind the bar from major league players. The thought made me sick. I couldn't do it. Those meant everything to my dad.

I walked to my office and sat down at my desk. The red X's on the calendar practically screamed at me. Knowing I had no other options, that was when I had texted Justin. To my surprise, he responded immediately that he was on his way.

Justin to the rescue. My dream had been right. He was going to save me. I just never thought it was going to be from a shady loan shark.

We had been texting for the past couple of days, ever since my sister showed up at my place. Cara had left early in the morning before I woke up. She didn't wake me up to say goodbye. She didn't leave a note. When I went downstairs, I found the blankets and towels folded on the couch. I tried calling her immediately, but of course she didn't answer. I was mad at myself for not demanding more answers when I had the chance. Now she was gone again, and I was still left with this mess.

The only good thing going on in my life were my conversations with Justin. They distracted me. I learned more about him and his family life. I was sad that he didn't have a great relationship with his father. I couldn't imagine hating my dad. But then again, every family had drama. Just look at me and my sister.

I learned more about his past. He was always the party boy and it didn't sound like he had been in a real relationship like ever. It wasn't that surprising. I knew he didn't want to settle down, but then he asked me on a date, which took me off guard. At first, I'll admit I was excited about the idea. Through our texts, I had really grown to like him. Plus, I already knew the physical aspect was there. Still, it took me a few minutes to think about it and ultimately respond with a no. There simply wasn't room in my life right now to explore the possibility of a relationship.

I thought he would stop talking to me after that, but he took the rejection well and we continued talking. I felt bad because I liked him and I definitely made that known with flirtatious texts and the occasional selfie. I was probably leading him on. Or maybe I just wanted him to wait for my life to be less complicated.

The fact that he dropped everything to come here now was a good sign. As much as I didn't want to accept his help, he was my last resort. Of course, I would demand a contract and terms of how to pay him back. I was not going to accept money without stipulations. I didn't want a handout. That wasn't who I was.

He would be here soon. I went to the bathroom to freshen up a bit. I smoothed my hair and put on a little lip gloss. I shrugged at my reflection in the mirror. This was as good as it was going to get.

As I left the bathroom, I heard a soft knock on the door. I opened it and saw him standing there in a charcoal suit and white shirt. Damn. I forgot how good he looked in a suit. I swallowed hard. I had the urge to pull him into my office again and forget the whole deal, but I thought better of it. I needed to keep my wits about me. This meeting was about business, not pleasure. We shouldn't mix the two.

"Are you going to let me in?" He looked at me curiously as I stood in the doorway taking him in.

"Oh shit. Yeah, come in." I moved aside and he strode past me, clutching his laptop.

I shut the door behind him and locked it.

"This way," I said, leading him to my office.

I took a seat in my desk chair and he sat across from me.

"Are you okay?" he asked warily.

The truth was, I felt lightheaded and nauseous. I wasn't sure if it was the pregnancy or not eating all day. I let out a breath and closed my eyes.

"Not really."

"Did your sister come back? Did Lenin?" he asked worriedly.

"No, no." I waved him off. "I went to the bank today to try and get a loan, but they thought I was a joke."

"You're not a joke."

"I *am* a joke. I'm a broke bar owner with nothing."

"That's not true, Bridget. Don't say that."

"Why are you even here?" I asked.

"Because I want to help you."

"Why? You don't owe me anything."

"No, but…"

"But what?" I asked.

"God, why do you have to be so stubborn?" he asked, shaking his head.

Suddenly, I felt really sick. I felt my face drain of color.

"Bridget. What's wrong?" He leaned forward and grabbed my hand.

"I'm just hungry. I forgot to eat."

"Let's get you something to eat, okay?" he said softly, grabbing my hand and leading me out to the bar.

We went to the kitchen and he rummaged through the fridge as I pulled myself to sit on the counter. I watched as he grabbed bread from the shelf and pastrami and mayo from the fridge. He made me a sandwich, eyeing me carefully as he did so. Why was he so nice? It was irritatingly hot.

"Here," he said, handing me the sandwich. "Eat."

"Well, aren't you bossy?" I asked as I took the sandwich.

My stomach growled. I *was* hungry. I took a big bite.

"Happy?" I raised my eyebrows at him.

"Yes." The corners of his lips turned up.

I finished the sandwich quickly, while Justin poured me a glass of water from the bar.

"Are you ready to talk business now?" he asked.

I nodded as I took the glass of water from his hands. *Ready as I'd ever be.*

194

He grabbed my hand and led me back to my office. His hand felt warm in mine. It was nice to be taken care of. I felt bad for being rude to him when he was just trying to help.

We sat down again.

"Okay, where were we?" he asked.

"Lenin needs the money in three days' time. I can't get a loan, and I'd prefer not to sell anything from the bar. So, what are my options?"

"Well, I don't have enough time to create a portfolio for you. To earn anything, we'd really need a month's time. We could make a quick turnaround in a few days, but I don't want to take that gamble."

I sat back in my chair and crossed my arms. "I have no idea what you're talking about."

"Okay, well let me simplify things. I'll give you the money."

"No." I shook my head adamantly.

"Like I said, stubborn." He leaned back in his chair annoyed.

"I can't just let you *give* me ten thousand dollars, Justin."

"Why not? It's nothing in the grand scheme of things."

I laughed out loud. "Are you kidding me?" I asked, my voice raising.

"I told you—"

"You're rich. I get it." I rolled my eyes.

"I didn't mean for it to come off that way."

"Didn't you?"

"Bridget, I just want to help. Why did you ask me to come here if you weren't going to let me?"

"Okay. I'll take the money, *but* I want a contract."

"That's not necessary."

"Yes, it is. If we are going to do this, we are going to do it my way."

Just listening to myself, I realized how stubborn I sounded. Oh well. He was still here and hadn't run away yet. He would have to get used to it.

"Fine."

"There are to be terms for me paying you back. I'm not just taking a handout."

"But—"

"No buts." I put my hand up.

He looked up at the ceiling clearly exasperated with me.

"It's non-negotiable," I said, solidifying my stance.

He looked back at me and ran his hands over his face. "You're something else, you know that?"

"So, I've been told."

I checked my phone for the time. Andy would be here any minute to help me open the bar. We would have to sort out the contract later. I stood up from my desk.

"I have to get the bar ready," I said.

196

He stood and gathered his things before stepping toward me. I smelled his cologne as his eyes looked down at me intently. Oh, God, what was he doing to me? I could not be distracted so easily by the charisma that oozed off him. Instead, I held out my hand in the small space between us. He looked down at my hand and furrowed his brow. Then he let out a breathy laugh before putting his hand in mine.

I shook it firmly. "Thank you."

"Goodbye, Bridget." He knelt down and kissed me on the cheek. His breath soft against my ear made me involuntarily close my eyes, as it crept across my whole body.

He turned and walked out the door of my office, leaving me practically paralyzed. I watched him walk out the door as Andy entered. They exchanged hellos and then he was gone.

"He came back for more already?" asked Andy when he saw me in the doorway of the office.

"You are the worst," I said, trying to hide my smile.

I joined him behind the bar and felt my mood instantly lift. This was the most relief I had in days. I finally had a solution to pay Lenin and get him out of my life, and hopefully my sister's life, for good. I should have accepted Justin's help a while ago. It would have saved me a lot of sleepless nights. I was forever indebted to him, especially since it would take me a while to pay him back.

Chapter 22

Justin

I opened the door to my condo and tossed my keys on the entryway table. The sun was beginning to set, casting an orange glow over the living room. I flicked on a lamp and walked to the bar area in the corner of the room. I pulled a tumbler from the shelf and filled it with whiskey stones, the familiar clinking ringing in my ears. I poured a generous serving and took a sip. The warmth ran down my throat as I drummed my fingers on the marble countertop.

My thoughts were all over the place after leaving Bridget at the bar. The woman was giving me whiplash with her mixed signals. And that stubbornness. I was exhausted from trying to keep up. I was just happy she finally accepted the money, but not without demanding a contract. Why couldn't she just accept it as a gift? I shook my head just thinking about how bullheaded she was. It was frustratingly sexy.

Grabbing my drink, I plopped down on the couch. I took another sip before placing it on the glass coffee table. I pulled my laptop onto me and turned it on. I had gone over enough contracts in business to know how to type one up.

Besides, it didn't have to be meticulous. I didn't even want to draw one up in the first place, but if it would make Bridget accept the money, then I would.

I opened a Word document and stared at the cursor blinking at me. My fingers hovered over the keys as I tried to figure out the terms. We hadn't really gone over that. She was just adamant she wanted a contract, but didn't discuss what she wanted on it. She wanted to pay me back, but there were different ways to do that. It didn't have to be strictly monetary.

An idea came to me as I finished the rest of my whiskey. It was ballsy, but the opportunity was there. Instead of a payment plan, she would agree to date me in exchange for the money I gave her. It was a win-win situation.

I had been wanting to ask her out again after being denied the first time. This would be a guarantee where she couldn't say no. It felt like we were practically dating anyway with how much time we spent texting each other and the intimacy we had already shared. If she would stop being so stubborn, she would see we were well on our way.

This would also be a way to protect myself. I had dated women in the past who were just interested in my money. They spun sticky webs, told me lies, tried to trap me. It was a wonder I didn't really trust women or want to settle down. From what I'd learned about Bridget, she didn't seem like that type of woman. Still, a contract would just offer me that peace of mind.

I began typing up the contract, all the while wondering how much it was going to piss her off when she read it over. With the deadline approaching, she didn't have much of a choice. She'd have to sign it.

Once I finished typing it, I looked it over briefly. It was a simple, single-page document. I hit *print*. As my laptop connected to my office printer, I poured myself another glass of whiskey. The sun had set now and the sky was a deep lilac color hovering over the city lights below. In that moment, I thought about the possibility of sharing these types of moments with Bridget soon.

I liked texting her. She was funny. The memes she sent always made me laugh. The selfies she sent were all favorited in my phone. But, I wanted more from her. The only place I really saw her was at the bar. Hell, the bar was the only place we'd had sex. I was ready to bring her to my place or see her. I wanted to take her to dinner or order takeout on the couch. Tomorrow I'd know if she would accept the deal or not.

My phone buzzed in my pocket. It was Bridget: *Hey.*

Me: *Hi.*

Bridget: *I just wanted to say sorry for being such a stubborn bitch earlier.*

Me: *Stubborn, yes. Bitch, no.*

Bridget: *Again, thank you for helping me.*

Me: *I want to. You know that. I'll bring the contract and the money tomorrow before the bar opens.*

Bridget: *Okay. I'll see you then.*

Me: *Have a good night at work.*

Bridget: *Thank you.*

I heard the printer beeping from my office. I walked in and pulled the paper from the tray. Under my desk light, I signed my name on the line. Tomorrow, we'd see if Bridget would sign hers underneath.

***

The next morning, I drove to the bank with my briefcase in hand.

"Good morning, Mr. Ralston," the teller greeted me.

Her name was Samantha. She was who I had signed an account with when I first moved to the city. She was a knockout. Straight black hair with caramel eyes and olive skin. She had offered to show me around the city, but I never took her up on the offer.

"Good morning. I'd like to get into my safety deposit box."

"Of course. May I have your ID, please? I know you, but it's procedure." She winked.

"I understand." I slid my ID from my wallet and handed it to her. She studied it for only a moment before handing it back to me.

"I'll go get your key and lead you back. Wait for the door to buzz and then you can enter."

I nodded and leaned against a nearby wall. Soon, the door buzzed and I pulled it open. Samantha led me to the safety deposit room and unlocked the door.

"I'll be just outside. Take your time, Mr. Ralston."

"Thank you, Samantha."

I lay my briefcase on a table and clicked it open. I took my key and opened my safety deposit box. Most all of my money was in the bank, except for a small amount I kept in here. It wasn't recommended, but I didn't need the bank reporting to the feds about my taking out such a large sum of money. I pulled out ten stacks of cash and placed them neatly in my briefcase. I clicked it shut and locked the box.

I met Samantha outside. She perked up when she saw me exit the room. She locked up behind me and began leading me to the front.

"So, how are you liking Boston?" she asked.

"Just fine. It's feeling much more like home."

"You know, you never did take me up on my offer."

I smiled sheepishly. "Oh right. I'm so sorry, but I'm actually seeing someone now."

I wasn't. Not yet, at least. After today, that was going to change.

"Well, she's a lucky girl." She gave me a tight-lipped smile.

I handed her my key and she led me out to the lobby. She gave me a quick wave goodbye before heading back behind the counter.

I immediately drove home. I didn't think it smart to wander the city with ten grand in my briefcase. I had a while before I was going to meet Bridget at the bar. Thankfully, I had a few meetings over video calls to kill time. I spent the rest of my time watching the stock market and making any trades that seemed profitable.

Just after 2 p.m., I drove over to Murphy's with the money and contract secure in my briefcase in the trunk of my car. I parked in an empty spot out front, retrieved the briefcase, and knocked on the door. After a moment, the door swung open and Bridget ushered me inside. She peered out front before shutting the door behind us.

"Just making sure that creep isn't around. I always feel like I'm being watched," she said warily as she locked the door.

"Has he been back?"

"No, but he sent one of his henchmen in last night. He left me a black business card with a simple phone number on it. I'm supposed to call it when the money is ready."

"Sounds totally legit," I said, trying to lighten the situation.

"Ugh. Come on," she said.

I noticed she was wearing a short jean skirt. It was different than her usual jeans or leggings. My eyes ran up her toned legs as she led me to her office. We had the place to ourselves. Andy wasn't there yet, which was probably good, considering this shady transaction about to take place.

She sat down in her desk chair and I sat across from her. This felt all too familiar to yesterday. I just hoped she wasn't as stubborn today. I placed my briefcase on her desk and clicked it open. I noticed her eyes widen as she saw the stacks of cash lined up neatly inside.

"Do you have somewhere safe to keep it?"

"I have a safe." She nodded toward the corner of the room. I only saw a small fridge.

I looked at it and back at her questioningly. She laughed.

"It looks like a fridge, but it's actually a safe that's nailed to the floor."

"Smart."

"I know." A satisfactory smile spread across her lips.

Then she looked at me intently. "Where's the contract? I'm not touching that money without one."

"I know, I know." I put my hands up in defense.

I pulled the paper from my briefcase. I slid it across the desk toward her. I held my breath as she picked it up. I hoped she wouldn't be angry, or worse, offended. I watched as her eyes read over the words printed before her.

She let out an exasperated laugh before looking at me.

"You've got to be joking?" she said, crossing her arms and leaning back in her chair.

"Actually, I'm completely serious."

"These weren't the terms I had in mind."

"We never discussed terms. You wanted a contract. There it is." I pointed at the paper in her hands.

She placed it on the desk and coolly slid it back to me. "I'm not agreeing to this."

"You kind of have to if you want the money." I shrugged.

"I don't want it then."

I let out an exasperated sigh and threw my hands up. We sat silently glaring at each other for a minute. This woman was going to make me pull out my hair one of these days. As I stared at her longer, I couldn't help the corners of my lips creeping up. She tried to hold a serious face, but failed. I shut my briefcase and stood. Her eyes watched me cautiously as I stepped toward her.

We weren't going to get to an agreement right now, but I knew the best way to distract her. I grabbed her hands and pulled her up from her chair so she was facing me. I tucked my finger under her chin and tilted her face up toward me. Her brow furrowed before she let go and her eyelids fluttered close. I leaned in and lightly pressed my lips to hers.

My hand slid to her lower back and pulled her against me swiftly. She let out a small gasp and I took my opportunity to slip my tongue in her mouth and massage it against hers. She moaned into me before pulling away suddenly.

"I know what you're doing," she said sharply.

I leaned in close and whispered in her ear, "And what's that?"

She leaned her head back and my lips brushed against her neck, planting soft kisses. "Distracting me."

"I don't know what you're talking about."

My hand ran slowly up her thigh and under the hem of her skirt. I trailed my fingers against her and she gave in. One day we would make it to my bed, but for now, our usual place would do.

Chapter 23

Bridget

I lay on top of Justin, totally spent, and totally naked. My head was on his chest, listening to his breathing as I looked around my office. We were on the floor in a tangled heap. I wondered how we always ended up here. How had we gone from going over a contract to save me from a loan shark to him being inside me? He had this irresistible power of me that was incredibly frustrating, but a turn-on just the same.

As we lay in silence, my mind went back to the contract. I couldn't believe the terms he had laid out. In exchange for money, we would have to date. It was the most ridiculous thing I had ever heard of, but a part of me wanted to do it. I knew I was being hardheaded about it and had initially refused before he distracted me. The truth was, I would be okay with seeing him more. More than okay actually.

I liked him. I tried to convince myself otherwise, but it was no use. Our conversations were easy. We already knew so much about each other. When I thought about him, I couldn't help but feel giddy, and giddy is *not* a word I use. Ever. He also made me feel safe and taken care of, which is something I hadn't felt in a long time. I was usually the one keeping everyone else safe and taken care of. It was a nice change.

I could also get used to the sex because every single time it got better. I didn't know how that was possible. We practically tore each other's clothes off earlier. We didn't take anything slow. There was no foreplay. There was a frantic desperation to be as close to one another as possible.

But even with all of that, there was one thing that was complicating the situation. The baby. I would have to tell him about it eventually. He would know something was up when the morning sickness hit full force. It had just begun and it was not pretty. Even if I could hide it, he would eventually notice my belly getting larger. My breasts were already growing more engorged, much to his liking. His hands and mouth were just all over them.

I could tell him now, but I was too scared. I'd had plenty of opportunities to tell him, but something always held me back. After I dealt with Lenin and fixed the mess that was my life, I'd tell him. I had already been keeping it from him. What was a little longer?

"You should go," I whispered as I rolled off him and lay on my back beside him.

"Oh?" He rolled onto his side and looked at me.

"I mean, I'd love for you to stay, but I have to open up the bar."

"Are you sure?" I felt his hand graze up my inner thigh and a small tremor rolled through me. He smiled at me deviously. A part of me considered letting him stay and having Andy open up, but I didn't want him to be here in case Lenin randomly showed up.

I leaned in and kissed him. "Don't you think we've tortured Andy enough?" I teased.

He laughed. "Poor guy."

I nipped his bottom lip with my teeth before sitting up. I reached for my clothes and started to get dressed.

"Fiiiiiine. I'll go." he said dramatically, as he grabbed his clothes.

After we were dressed, I peeked out of my office door. Andy wasn't there yet. Thank God. I opened the door wider.

"Coast is clear," I said.

I led Justin to the door, but before I opened it, he grabbed my hand.

"Let me know what happens, okay? With Lenin. I don't like this at all. I don't want anything to happen to you."

"I'll be fine." I squeezed his hand before pushing the door open.

Justin gave me a small wave before walking to his car and driving away. I closed the door and locked it before going back to my office.

I opened my desk drawer and found the black card that Lenin's guy had left.

I dialed the number and left a message. "I have your money. Come by the bar tomorrow morning."

I hung up just as I heard Andy unlock the door and walk in. I was relieved to have someone here with me, just in case. This was all almost over.

Later that night, I was pouring shots for a large party when I heard the bar fall silent, except for Lynyrd Skynyrd playing. I looked up and saw my sister stumbling through the door. She looked disheveled, her hair a tangled mess and in the same clothes as when she stayed at my place.

I rushed toward her. "Cara!" I grabbed her arms to steady her. I winced at the smell. She reeked of alcohol.

"Let go of me!" she pushed me off her as everyone around us watched with their mouths open.

I grabbed her arm again and pulled her toward the bar. I sat her down on a barstool. She swayed and grabbed hold of the bar top to not fall. I noticed more bruises on her face and arms.

"Andy, water. Please," I said desperately.

Andy quickly grabbed a glass, filling it with ice and water. He handed it to me worriedly.

"Have some water, Cara," I said calmly.

She smacked it out of my hand, the glass falling and shattering on the floor. I felt everyone's eyes on us, but tried to ignore their stares. This was not the good time they had come here for. I had to get Cara under control.

"Cara, calm down," I said, my voice low.

"I don't want to calm down," she spat in my face.

"You're making a scene."

"Oh, boo hoo. Sorry for making a scene in your precious bar."

"I just think you need to sober up a little. Let me take care of you."

"Oh, *now* you want to take care of me?" She laughed.

"I always do, but sometimes you just make it so hard."

"I'm sorry your life is *so* hard," she slurred.

"Do you even know the mess you've caused me?" I felt anger fluttering in my stomach.

"Poor little Bridget," said Cara sarcastically. "What about the mess you've caused *me?*"

"Are you joking?"

"Look at my life compared to yours."

"I'm not to blame for the way your life turned out. You made your own choices."

"Maybe if I was Daddy's favorite, I would have gotten this place. But no, perfect Bridget got everything served to her on a silver platter." Cara waved her arm around.

"I worked my ass off for this place," I snapped. "You know that. You barely stepped

212

foot in this place. It doesn't mean anything to you."

"Just like I don't mean anything to you. Or Dad."

"Get out," I whispered. I had heard enough. After everything we had done for her over the years. Enough was enough.

"Andy, get security," I said, looking away from her.

"Um, are you sure?" asked Andy, looking between us both.

"Yes. Do it."

"Are you seriously kicking me out?" asked Cara angrily.

"Yes. I am. It's for your own good, Cara."

"I hate you," she said with bated breath.

"Well, in this moment, the feeling's mutual."

He walked to the front door and motioned for the doorman to come in. I watched with my arms crossed as he dragged my sister from the bar. She tried to fight back, throwing punches, but he was too strong for her. He linked his arms under hers and basically dragged her out as the entire bar looked on. Despite my tough exterior, internally I was falling apart.

I wanted to believe that if I kept helping my sister, she would get her life together. But no matter how many times I bailed her out or solved her problems for her, she was always going to be

Cara. Her showing up here tonight was proof of that.

It pained me to see that she had been roughed up. I wondered if Lenin had been behind it. The thought of it made me sick with worry. I suddenly felt nauseous. I ran to the bathroom and threw up in the stall. I steadied myself on the toilet as I processed everything that had just happened.

I groaned as I held my head against the toilet, trying to ignore it was a public restaurant. I held my stomach with one hand, trying to soothe myself. There was a baby in there. That was the first moment that it felt real. I had a little boy or girl growing inside of me. I felt a rush of love wash over me. Alongside it was worry. How was I going to protect my child with this chaos around me? Chaos that only came with my sister being around.

I knew I had to choose. I could either keep letting Cara back into my life, or I could protect my baby and myself. As hard as it would be, I knew I had to cut ties. I could no longer enable my baby sister.

A moment later, I heard a soft knock at the door.

"Um, Bridget. Are you okay?" Andy's voice drifted into the women's restroom.

"I'm good. I'll be right out."

"Okay…"

I took a deep breath and pulled myself to stand. I washed my hands and rinsed my mouth out at the sink. How would I ever know if these were pregnancy-induced symptoms or Cara-induced symptoms? I dried my hands off and pushed the door open where I found Andy cautiously waiting.

"Who is manning the bar?" I asked, looking around.

"No one. I wanted to check on you. Everyone out there, including me, is worried about you."

"I'm fine. Really. Thank you for taking care of *that.*" I looked toward the door.

"Jason made sure she got an Uber to take her... somewhere."

"Thank you, Andy. Really." I gave him a quick hug. "We have to get back to work."

When we walked back behind the bar, everyone fell silent as they eyed me warily. I felt my face turn red.

Andy gave me a pat on the back. "Are you sure you don't want to take a breather in your office, or go lay down in the loft even?" he asked softly.

I shook my head. "I'm fine. Thank you."

Then I turned to everyone and made an announcement. "The show is over. I'm sorry you had to see that. Please accept my apology for the disruption."

"It's okay, Bridget," shouted a customer.

"We've got you, girl," shouted another.

This was my family. I felt relief wash over me in that moment. Murphy's was my home and I would do anything to protect it. I loved these people.

"Thank you. Please accept a round of drinks from me. On the house," I said, forcing a smile.

The bar erupted into cheers and fists pumped in the air. The silence was over and the party was back on. As I looked around, I wished Justin was here. I kicked myself for sending him away. I didn't know why I did it or why I kept him at arm's length, when he clearly wanted to be closer. I think I just wanted to protect myself.

Despite the dream I had of him slaying the dragon and saving me, I wanted to be able to save myself. It was my strong, stubborn side. My dad had raised me like that. I was never taught to be a damsel in distress, like in my dream. I was taught to fight. That was what I was doing. I didn't need to drag anyone else down with me. Even though Justin generously helped me, I wanted to ride the rest of this out alone.

Chapter 24

Justin

I paced my living room, looking down at the city below. I was waiting for an update from Bridget. It was one a.m. Lenin must have shown up by now for the exchange. I had texted her an hour ago, but I didn't get a response. I kept telling myself she was probably busy running the bar, but worry still crept in at the corners of my mind.

Grabbing my phone from my pocket, I texted her again: Hey. *Just checking in. Again. Please text me back.*

I knew I sounded desperate, and I was.

I waited ten minutes, but she didn't text back.

With a sigh, I tossed my phone on the couch. I plopped down next to it and ran my fingers through my hair in frustration. I knew she wanted to handle this on her own, which had to be part of the reason why she wanted me to leave earlier this afternoon. At least she had the money. Maybe I had done all I could do for her.

But if she expected me not to worry, then she was mistaken. The idea of her handling a shady loan shark made my stomach bubble with unease. I knew nothing about this guy. He could be dangerous or violent. Maybe he had been the one who had roughed up Bridget's sister. What if he laid a hand on Bridget? The thought filled me with rage.

My attempt to sleep off my worry earlier failed miserably, which was why I was now pacing in the dark with horrible thoughts running through my mind. I couldn't stay here. I had to go see if she was okay.

I stood quickly from the couch and snatched my keys off the entry table. I jogged down to the parking garage and got in my car. I sped to the bar, but it felt like I was going five miles per hour.

I wasn't going to let her do this alone. No one knew she was in this mess besides me and her sister. Her sister surely wasn't going to protect her. She was the one who had gotten her into this tangled web. I needed to be there for her if anything went wrong.

The bar looked packed when I pulled up. People stood outside, waiting to get in. It made me feel a little more at ease knowing she was surrounded by people if Lenin had come in. I knew Andy would be here, but he didn't seem like much of a fighter. I scanned the area for a parking spot, but didn't find one. I drove up and down the street until I found a metered spot about two blocks away. I walked swiftly down the sidewalk to the bar.

I pulled the door open and loud music hit my ears. My eyes adjusted to the dim lighting and I saw people everywhere. I scanned the bar for Bridget. I just saw Andy behind the bar. My stomach dropped. I pushed through the crowd toward the bar.

"Andy! Where is Bridget?" I called out.

"Hey, Justin!" he shouted over the music.

"Where is Bridget?" I asked again.

"Huh?" He couldn't hear me.

"Bridget! Where is she?" I yelled.

"Oh, she's in the bathroom. Is everything okay?" he asked, eyeing me curiously.

"Yeah, I just need to talk to her."

"Do you want a drink while you wait?" he asked.

"No, that's okay." I shook my head. I wanted my head clear for this transaction. I needed to be on my toes if anything went awry.

"You missed one hell of a show," he said, sliding me a glass of water instead.

"What do you mean?" I asked. Had Lenin already shown up? Was I too late? Why hadn't Bridget texted me back to let me know she was okay?

"Cara, Bridget's sister, showed up here. A total mess. She caused this big scene."

"Where is she now? Was she with anyone?" I asked, looking around the bar. Maybe she had come with her loan shark friend.

"Nah, she was by herself. She was a total shitshow though. Totally wasted. She said some nasty things to Bridget, and Bridget called security on her."

"Really?" I was shocked.

"Yeah, I know. I'm proud of Bridg, though. That sister of hers is always causing her trouble. It's about time she cut the cord. Some people can't be helped."

I nodded and glanced around the bar. Just then, Bridget emerged from the side hallway of the bathrooms. I walked quickly toward her. When she saw me, she looked surprised and then something else washed over her face. I didn't feel welcome all of a sudden. My stomach sank.

"What are you doing here?" she asked, looking me up and down with a raised brow.

I looked down and noticed I was in my pajamas. I left my place in such haste because I was so worried that I didn't bother to change. It didn't matter, though. I was just glad I was here.

"You never texted me back," I said.

"Um hello. I'm working. I run this place, remember?"

"Yeah, but I was worried."

"Well, you don't have to be." She shrugged and avoided my gaze.

"Bridget. What is going on?"

I didn't know why she was being like this.

"Andy, I'll be right back. Can you man the bar?" she asked, rapping her knuckles on the bar top.

"Yeah. Sure thing."

"Come on," Bridget said to me, gesturing for me to follow her.

She lifted the bar counter and walked toward the kitchen. She walked through the kitchen, past the cooks making late-night nachos and loaded fries, and pushed open the door to the back alley. The air was cool and crisp.

She suddenly turned to look at me, crossing her arms.

"I thought you got the hint earlier," she said sharply.

"I'm sorry?"

"This afternoon."

"This afternoon was amazing. Did I miss something?"

She sighed heavily. "Yeah, it was fun and all..."

"Fun..." I repeated slowly.

That's all? I thought it was more than that.

Here I was, thinking what we had was something more. At least I hoped it would get there. Now she was making it seem like I was just some glorified booty call.

"But I asked you to leave, Justin. So why are you back here again?"

"Bridget, I came here to make sure you were okay. I was worried about you. You have ten thousand dollars sitting in your office and some dangerous guy who is coming to get it."

"The money is safe, and I will handle it when he gets here. I thought I told you I wanted to do this on my own."

A part of me was relieved to hear that he hadn't come yet, but she was pushing me away. Again. How many times did we have to go through this?

"I don't want you to have to do it on your own. Bridget, I care about you. I don't know what I would do if anything happened to you."

"You barely know me," she snapped.

"I do know you. You love sappy movies. You prefer whiskey to wine. You order chai tea lattes. You got that scar on your knee from riding your bike down the steep hill on the corner by your old house."

"Listing off a few random facts doesn't mean you know me."

"I know you're stubborn as hell, much to my demise, but you're a softie deep down too. Your heart is too big and it can sometimes be your downfall with some of the people in your life."

"Will you just stop?" she said loudly.

I stopped talking as her eyes glared at me. We stood in silence for a moment.

"Why are you doing this?" she asked quietly, looking at something off at the distance.

"What?"

"Complicating things."

"Because I want to be with you?"

"Yes, I don't need this in my life right now. I don't need you. You're the one who told me you didn't want to settle down. You physically shuddered at the thought. Don't you remember?"

"Yes, but things have changed. I've changed."

She laughed out loud. It was hostile and cut through me.

"You're a party boy, Justin. A player. Don't kid yourself."

She was taking my past and using it against me. I couldn't believe it. We had opened up to each other and shared parts of ourselves, the good and the bad. I had trusted her with that.

"Maybe I was, but not anymore. Bridget, I want to be with you. I thought maybe you wanted the same."

"Well, you thought wrong."

"Look, I know you said you didn't want to settle down either, but there's something here. You see that, don't you?" I stepped toward her and reached for her hands, holding them between us.

"There's nothing here, Justin. I'm sorry," she said softly, pulling her hands away and crossing her arms.

I gave a single nod. I had clearly read things wrong with her. Everything we had shared over the past few months was a lie.

"What was it all for then?" I asked softly, searching her eyes for answers.

"Don't you get it?" she asked as if I was dumb.

I shook my head.

"Money. I needed money. I saw my chance and took it."

"That's not true," I said sharply.

"Yes, it is. You think I don't know a rich, pretty boy when I see one?"

I didn't believe her.

"You're lying."

"I'm not. Cleo told me what you did for a living, and you didn't do much to hide it. You flaunted it with your fancy suit and your shiny briefcase. You went on and on about your business and how successful you are, and how daddy left you a nice little trust fund. God, my ears nearly bled just listening to how full of yourself you are."

"Stop," I said under my breath. I didn't want to hear any more.

"It's no wonder your parents want nothing to do with you. You're a spoiled, pretentious little boy."

I felt like she had just slapped me across the face. My eyes started to burn, but I sure as hell wasn't going to let her see me cry. I had never in my life cried in front of a woman. She wasn't about to be the first. I was humiliated, but most of all hurt. She had been throwing daggers all night, but this one she twisted into me.

She turned out to be just like every other woman, and I had walked right into her trap. I felt embarrassed for talking about my wealth to her. I knew better than that. I kicked myself for it, but also for opening up to her about everything about my family. Those wounds were fresh, and she had just torn them wide open again.

"Good luck, Bridget."

I turned my back to her and took a deep breath. I could feel her eyes on me. I began to walk away. I needed to get out of there. Before I exited the alley, I turned.

"You can have the money. No contract. No terms. No strings attached. I want nothing to do with you."

Then I turned the corner and walked to my car. I felt like crying. I felt like throwing up. I was in shock over what had just happened with the woman I had begun to fall for. I didn't even recognize her back there. She was venomous, hitting me where it hurt. I felt like an absolute fool.

When I reached my car, I shakily put the key in the ignition and turned it on. It roared to life, and I sat in the driver's seat wondering where to go. Without any clue of where I would end up, I put the car into drive and sped away. I watched the bar fade to a speck in my rearview mirror.

Goodbye, Bridget.

Chapter 25

Bridget

After Justin rounded the corner out of sight, I doubled over and burst into tears. I had hurt him. Badly. There was probably no coming back from that. How could there be?

He wasn't supposed to show up here tonight. I didn't want him any more involved in this mess than he already was. He was too good a man to drag down with me. That was why I needed him to leave, and the only way to do that was to hurt him.

I didn't mean any of the words I had said to him. It pained me to shoot that kind of venom at him, especially after he had opened up to me in such a way. It was almost like I was having an out-of-body experience, watching myself say such vile lies to him. I had never spewed such hatred in my life, but I had to. It was the only way he would actually leave. It was for his own good.

He didn't want to be with me. He probably just liked the idea of rescuing me and that was no way to start a relationship. A relationship he told me he had no interest in with anyone. You don't just change your mind like that, especially for a washed-up bar owner on the verge of losing everything.

It took everything in me not to fall into his arms when he was pouring his heart out to me. It all felt too good to be true. He knew me. The real me. Despite how different we were, we could be good together and that terrified me. I had never met anyone like him before, and if there was a chance I let him in, there was a chance I could lose him. I didn't think I could bear falling in love with him just to have him leave.

I could have told him about the baby, but I was too scared to. He would probably tell me more of what I wanted to hear. That he would keep us safe. That he would take care of us. How would I know if he really meant it or was just saying it because he had to?

I stood up warily. I couldn't stay in this alley forever thinking about things that no longer mattered. Justin was gone, and it was for the best. I had too much going on in my life for relationship issues.

"Get it together, Bridg," I whispered to myself.

I attempted to put myself back together in the darkness of the alley. I hoped the bar was dim enough for people not to notice my red, swollen eyes. God, this whole night had been a mess. First, my sister showing up and causing an embarrassing scene. Then, Justin showing up when I just wanted him to stay away. Now, I had never felt more alone.

I pulled open the door to the kitchen. The cooks were cleaning up the counters and stove. They were done serving food for the night because we were so close to closing. I gave them a forced smile and pushed open the swinging doors to the bar.

The place was still surprisingly packed. Andy was moving quickly, pouring drinks and unloading clean glasses. I felt bad for leaving him on his own. I sidled up beside him and began placing clean glasses on the counter.

"I'm sorry I left you. Thank you for letting me deal with…that," I said.

"It's okay. How was *that?*" he asked.

"It's over."

"Oh, Bridg…" He put his arm on my back.

"Don't," I said, holding my hand up. I didn't need anyone's sympathy for a relationship that never started. Plus, I didn't want to break down again thinking about it.

I checked my watch. It was nearly 2 a.m.

"We should probably do last call."

He nodded, looking as if he wanted to say more, but didn't. Instead, he cupped his hands around his mouth and shouted, "Last call! If you're still thirsty, this is your last chance!"

The next five minutes were a madhouse with everyone ordering their last drinks for the night. Once security escorted the last customer out the door, he gave me a wave and clocked out for the night. Poor guy had quite the night dealing with my sister earlier. She was like a wild animal.

Looking at the empty bar, I wondered why Lenin hadn't shown up. I had left that message to let him know I was ready for the exchange. Now the bar was closed and I guessed I had to wait another day. I really had hoped this would all be behind me after tonight.

I walked to the door and looked outside, but no one was there. I sighed as I locked the door behind him and began wiping down the tables. Andy stood behind the bar counting tips, eyeing me as he did so. I knew he had a lot of questions about everything, but I didn't want to talk about it. Not right now.

"Hey, after you're done with that, you can head out."

"What? Are you sure?" He looked around the bar warily. There was still a lot to do, but I would rather do it alone with my thoughts.

"I'm sure."

"Okay. Thanks, boss." He started counting a little faster. Soon, he had split the tips and was hanging up his apron.

"You sure you're going to be okay? It was an eventful night for you," he said.

"I'll be fine. I always am."

He nodded solemnly before disappearing through the kitchen. It was so quiet without the music and the chattering of customers. I took my time wiping down the tables and chairs. I cleaned the beer taps and emptied the trash cans. I shook out the mats and swept the floors. The mindless work was good for me. It helped distract me from my thoughts, which were annoyingly trying to creep in.

Once I was finished, I unlocked my office door. I spotted the contract folded on my desk. I picked it up and read over it once more. The terms were ridiculous, but they didn't even matter anymore. Justin said I could have the money. No strings attached. It felt wrong.

I strode over to the safe and made sure it was locked. I would figure out what to do about it later. Since Lenin didn't show up tonight, that meant I had more time to maybe find a different solution. I turned the lights off and locked my office door behind me.

I walked back to the kitchen and yawned as I hung up my apron. I was exhausted, both mentally and physically. I went down the long panel of lights for the bar, flicking them off one by one. Lastly, I grabbed my purse and set the alarm at the back door. I stepped out into the quiet of the night. Everyone was fast asleep by now.

As I rummaged through my purse for my car keys, I thought I heard footsteps. I looked around quickly, but was only met with darkness.

Finding my keys, I quickly pulled them from my purse and walked swiftly to my car.

Suddenly, I felt a hand cover my lips. A muffled scream escaped my mouth as another hand wrapped around my waist and pulled me firmly against my attacker. I struggled to break free, but their hold tightened around me. My eyes looked around frantically. Someone stepped out from the shadows of a nearby dumpster and walked slowly toward me. I squinted trying to see.

It was Lenin. His mouth was curled into a smile that didn't meet his eyes.

"It's nice to see you again, Ms. Quinn," he said.

I tried to speak, but couldn't.

"I'm going to ask Jared to let you go now, but if you try and run or scream, it will end badly. Do you understand?"

I slowly nodded. I was released and the hand over my mouth pulled away. I sucked in a long, shaky breath.

"Your sister. Where is she?" asked Lenin.

"I-I don't know," I stammered.

"I don't believe you." He took a step toward me.

"I promise. She was here tonight, but I kicked her out. I don't know where she went."

Lenin studied my face as if he was searching for a lie. He pressed his lips into a grim line. He seemed to believe me.

"Look, I have your money," I said. "All of it. Please, just let me get it for you and this all can be over. You can leave me and my sister alone."

"Ahhh, but I'm not interested in that anymore."

"Wh-what? I got you the money in time!" I said in disbelief.

Lenin rubbed his fingertips together as he looked at me thoughtfully. "Yes, but I realized you're worth more than a mere ten thousand."

I didn't understand what he was talking about. This was not what we had agreed to. What was he playing at? I looked around helplessly for anyone to come save me.

"You're all alone, sweetheart. Now, you're gonna come with me." He nodded to Jared, who stood behind me. Lenin began walking toward a black town car I hadn't noticed earlier. I felt Jared's arms wrap around me tightly as he started to drag me after Lenin. I kicked and flailed about and let out a scream. Suddenly, Lenin whipped around and backhanded me across the face. My cheek stung as I bit my lip not to cry.

"I warned you," he said before turning to continue walking. He unlocked the car door.

"Why are you doing this?" I asked frantically.

"Because I know that Richie Rich you've been hanging with is gonna come save you. Then I'll get my money and more," Lenin said as he opened the car door.

Oh my God. Lenin watched with satisfaction as the look of realization crossed my face.

"Smart, ain't it?" he asked, leaning in closely.

Lenin must have been following me. I knew I had seen him lurking about. He knew about Justin. The thought made my stomach sink. After everything I had wanted to avoid, I had still put him in danger. My eyes stung with tears. Jared shoved me toward the car.

"Get in the car, sweetheart. Or Jared will put you there."

"Please! You can't do this!" I grabbed Lenin's arm.

He looked down at my hand and pulled it off, finger by finger. "I can actually."

"You don't understand. I'm pregnant!"

He looked taken aback for a split second, but then an evil smile crossed his lips. "Then you're probably worth even more."

I watched helplessly as he walked around to the passenger seat and slid inside the car. I felt Jared standing behind me, his hand on the open back door.

"Are you getting in, or not?" he asked impatiently.

I didn't see any other choice. I had to follow their commands—I saw what they had most likely done to my sister and needed to protect the baby. Slowly, I slid into the car, jumping as the door slammed loudly behind me. Jared clambered into the driver's seat and turned the car on. Lenin said something to him, but I couldn't hear. He slowly pulled out of the back alley to the bar. I kept my eyes straight ahead, trying to keep my breathing slow. Despite this, my mind was going a million miles per hour.

I didn't know where they were taking me. I didn't know what was going to happen. I just hoped Justin wouldn't come for me. I didn't deserve that. Not after I had hurt him so badly. There didn't look to be another way out of this. I leaned my head against the backseat, and let the tears fall silently.

Chapter 26

Justin

I sat in the driver's seat with the car running as I looked out over the empty park. The night was dark, no moon in the sky. It somehow made me aware of how alone I was.

After I had left Bridget, I just drove around the city. I ended up at this park. It was one I hadn't been to before. I thought it best not to go to the one where I had run into Bridget. Better not to go someplace with memories.

I was still reeling from what had happened earlier. The Bridget I had walked away from was not the Bridget I knew. She was unrecognizable. The emptiness in her eyes. Her cold attitude. Her hateful words. It felt like someone had shattered my heart into a thousand pieces.

I dropped my head to the steering wheel and closed my eyes. I had been a fool to think I had found a woman who was different, when in reality she was just the same as everyone else. I really had thought I found someone to settle down with. I didn't know it was what I wanted until I met Bridget.

Kenny had always chided me, saying it was time to grow up and find someone to spend my life with. I always brushed it off. Then I thought I found her—and she ruined me. Why did I think I could have what Kenny had? That was like a one-in-a-million chance for him. It was stupid to think it could happen to me too.

Maybe I was just a spoiled, pretentious, little boy, as she so nicely put it. I had practically set myself up for that, talking about my wealth and my trust fund. What was I thinking? I just wanted to assure her that I could help her. That I wanted to help her.

I gripped the steering wheel tighter, just going over everything in my mind. The money. The contract. What the hell was I thinking? Did I really think forcing a woman into a relationship through terms and conditions was a good idea? If I really thought about it, I wasn't serious. I just wanted her to take the money. If I got a date out of it, then great. I thought maybe I could convince her we were good together.

Now I realized we would never be good, let alone together. As much as I thought we were on the same page, I realized we weren't even in the same book. The only thing that made me feel better was knowing she had the money in her safe. At least she would be out of this mess with the loan shark, and I wouldn't have to worry about her anymore. Despite what she said to me, I still worried. I still wanted to protect her. It was stupid, I know.

Just then, my phone trilled in the cupholder beside me. I thought that was odd, considering it was nearly 4 a.m. Who would be calling at this hour? I picked it up quickly and saw Bridget's number flashing on the screen.

I waited a moment. A part of me wanted to not answer it. A part of me wanted to be petty. She deserved it after what she put me through back there. After everything she said, what could she possibly be calling me for? I decided to put my pettiness aside and find out. Maybe she was calling to apologize.

I hit the answer button.

"Hello?" I asked curtly.

"Justin Ralston?" a man's voice said on the other line.

The hair on the back of my neck and arms stood up straight. What the hell was going on? I pulled my phone away and checked the caller ID again. Maybe I had read it wrong. But no, it said it was a call from Bridget's phone.

"Uh, who is this?" I asked hesitantly.

"Don't ask questions."

My breath quickened.

The man spoke again. "I want triple what Ms. Quinn owes me."

"Who is this?" I demanded.

"I said, don't ask questions," the man barked.

It had to be Lenin. The exchange must have happened or had been attempted, but now he wanted more. I knew I shouldn't have left Bridget to deal with this on her own. No matter how much she hurt me, I should have fought to stay. I just hoped she was okay.

"Where is she?" I asked frantically.

I heard some rustling in the background and a woman yell out. It was Bridget. My heart jumped to my throat. He had her. She was in danger.

"What did I say about asking questions?" the man asked. "Now listen to me, Mr. Ralston. I want thirty thousand dollars tomorrow. Otherwise, your girlfriend and her baby will be hurt. Do you understand?"

I was seething. My vision was blurring in and out. I was seeing red. It took everything in me not to mouth off at the man on the phone. Knowing Bridget was there was the only thing stopping me. I had to keep her safe, and that meant going along with what Lenin demanded.

"I'll get you the money," I said.

"Good. Now you're playing the game," he said, amused.

"Thirty thousand."

"Correct. Bring it to the strip mall at the south end at 10 a.m."

I heard a click on the other line. I looked at my phone. He had hung up. I felt completely helpless. I knew nothing about this man or where he could be. I just knew he was dangerous and that he had Bridget.

I put my seatbelt on and put my car into drive, peeling out of the parking lot. I looked at the clock on my dash. I had six hours until I had to meet him with the money. The bank didn't open until 9 a.m. What the hell was I going to do in the meantime? I needed a plan.

I drove straight home and called Kenny. I didn't care how early it was.

"Hello?" he asked groggily, picking up after three rings.

"Kenny. Wake up!" I said loudly.

"Justin? What time is it?" I heard him rustling in bed. "Jesus, man. It's not even 5 a.m. What the hell?" he asked, stifling a yawn.

"Bridget is in trouble."

"What are you talking about?" he asked, sounding more alert.

I heard Cleo's voice in the background. "Kenny. Baby. What's going on?" she asked quietly.

"It's Justin. Something's going on with Bridget," Kenny said to her.

"Kenny, listen to me," I pleaded. "Bridget is in danger. She got involved with a loan shark. A really shady guy. He's dangerous. Her sister owed him money, but he came after Bridget."

"Oh, my God."

"I had lent her the money to pay him, but now he wants more. He has her, Kenny. He has Bridget." My voice broke.

"Okay, okay. Calm down. We will figure this out."

I took a deep breath.

"When does he need the money?" asked Kenny calmly.

"He needs thirty grand by 10 a.m. I'm meeting him at that strip mall at the south end."

"You're not going alone. I'll make some calls. They won't know what's coming."

I thought back to what Lenin said. He never said anything about coming alone. I didn't want to put Bridget in any danger by pissing him off, but I knew it was foolish to come without reinforcements. Kenny had an entire team of tough ball players who would back me up. I hated putting anyone in danger, but I would for Bridget.

"Okay. What do I do in the meantime?"

"Stay put. Don't do anything rash. Go to the bank when they open and we will meet you at the strip mall. She will be okay, Justin."

"I hope so," I said quietly.

"She will. I gotta go. I gotta make some calls."

"Okay. Thanks, Kenny."

I hung up and let out a long breath through my lips. I looked around my condo helplessly. I felt useless. There was nothing I could do but wait. I could go to the strip mall now, but there was a chance they wouldn't be there. And if they were, showing up empty-handed would only piss her captor off more.

I grabbed my laptop from the coffee table and began searching the internet. I only had Lenin's first name to go by and it wasn't like he was really advertising himself on the internet. I searched the web for an hour, but came up with nothing.

Then an idea came to me. Cara, Bridget's sister. She had to know more about this guy she had gotten into business with. I searched her up on the internet, but just found an old Facebook page. Since I wasn't her friend, I couldn't access much, but I did go through her profile pictures. I found one of her and Bridget hugging at the pier. Their smiles wide and their hair windswept. My heart skipped a beat when my eyes fell on Bridget. I couldn't lose her.

When 8:15 came around, I was still in the pajamas I had worn to the bar. I quickly changed into jeans and a T-shirt, and headed out the door. I got to the bank early and waited in the parking lot for them to open. I tapped my fingers impatiently on the steering wheel.

My phone buzzed in my pocket. I quickly grabbed it. It was Kenny.

"Hello?"

"We're set for the exchange. Two of the biggest guys on the team will meet us in the parking lot of the strip mall. When I told them about Bridget, they were raring to go. You know they love her from the bar. Everyone does."

"Yeah," I said, trying to keep it together.

"We've got this, man. We're going to get her out of there."

"Okay."

"Park on the east end of the lot. Far from the mall. I don't want them to be suspicious if several cars roll up," he said.

"Good idea. Okay. I'm at the bank now. I'll see you soon."

I hung up and watched as the security guards unlocked the door to the bank. I shut my car off and strode quickly through the door. I saw Samantha behind the counter. She looked up when she saw me, surprised I was the first customer there.

"Mr. Ralston. You're here bright and early," she said cheerfully.

"Samantha. I need to withdraw a large sum of money," I said.

She looked at me warily.

"Is everything okay? Are you in any trouble?" she asked, her brows furrowing as she looked around.

I didn't want to raise anyone's suspicions or get the law involved. I had to calm down.

"Oh no. I'm fine. Yeah. Everything is fine," I said casually. "I just have a buddy's bachelor party in Vegas tonight, and I need some gambling money."

I hoped the lie worked.

"How much do you need?" she asked, typing on the computer.

She bought it.

"Uh, like thirty thousand," I said, shrugging like it was nothing.

She looked at me and her eyes widened. I smiled at her convincingly.

"Sounds like a party," she said. "You'll have to fill out some additional paperwork because it's such a large sum."

"Not a problem, but can we make it speedy? I have a flight to catch."

"Of course." She turned to rummage through papers in a filing cabinet behind her.

I tapped my foot on the floor as I waited at the counter for her to bring the paperwork. I didn't have that type of money in my safe deposit box. I would have to take it out of my account. I'd have to answer questions later, but I didn't care. I had to get to Bridget. He said he would hurt her. Then it hit me and my knees buckled. He said he would hurt her and her *baby*. Was she…pregnant?

Chapter 27

Bridget

My legs were getting restless as I sat crammed in the backseat of the town car. The driver's seat was thoughtlessly pushed back and pressing against my knees. I knew my comfort wasn't these criminals' top priority. Hell, they'd kidnapped me. I had been terrified at first, obviously, but now we had been driving for hours and I was indifferent.

I looked out the window, stifling a yawn. We had been driving aimlessly around the city. The sun was up now, its rays fighting to peek through the clouds above. I wondered if they even had a well thought out plan. I wondered if they knew what to do with me. It was hard to hear their conversation from the backseat.

The smell of stale cigars kept wafting in my nostrils, making me want to throw up. I needed fresh air. Being pregnant was not helping. Every smell and swerve on the road made me queasy. I reached for the button on the door to roll down the window, but it didn't open. It must have been child locked or something. I wondered if I'd ever get out of this situation to worry about such car settings for the baby growing inside me.

"Can you please roll down the window? I need some fresh air," I asked, leaning forward to make sure they heard me.

"No can do, sweetheart," said Lenin.

"Then you won't mind if I throw up in the backseat," I said curtly.

Lenin thought for a moment before giving me an irritated look. He nodded to Jared. My window opened halfway and I sucked in the fresh air that blew toward me. It was sweet relief.

"No funny business back there. I have my eye on you," said Jared as he eyed me cautiously through the rearview mirror.

I avoided his gaze and continued to look out the window. I knew better than to piss these guys off. My cheek was still tender from where I was slapped earlier. It was better to listen, for my sake, but more importantly, for the baby's sake.

"So, is the baby Ralston's?" asked Lenin, turning to look at me with amused curiosity.

"That's none of your business," I snapped.

He laughed. "It is, actually. It means you're worth more to me than I thought."

"What kind of person kidnaps a pregnant woman?" I shot back.

"The kind who was screwed over by your stupid little sister," he sneered.

"She was stupid to get involved with someone like you," I mumbled, looking out the window.

246

"Judging from last night, you two don't have a pretty relationship. What kind of person kicks their own sister out of their establishment?"

My eyes shot back to Lenin. Had he been there? I surely would have seen him. It felt eerie to know a stranger had been watching me and knew about my life.

He must have seen the surprise in my eyes.

"I've been watching you for some time, Miss Quinn." He smiled and turned back around.

He *had* been watching me. And Justin. I thought I had been paranoid the past few weeks, but my senses were right. Had he been staking out others in my life? My mind immediately went to my dad. Was he in danger? I didn't dare ask and put any ideas in their heads. I shut my eyes tight, trying to block out the thought. Another wave of nausea rolled over me.

After a few minutes, when my stomach and mind settled, I looked around the car and observed my captors. I needed to know more about them, if there was some way I could get the upper hand on them. It was a laughable idea, but I had to try.

Lenin sat rigid in the front seat. Up close, his suit looked freshly pressed. His greasy hair was receding. I noticed a few gold fillings when he spoke to his henchman. He wore a watch that cost more than my car, but no wedding ring. That wasn't surprising.

247

Jared was huge with a bald head. He wore a much shabbier suit than Lenin, as if he was trying to be something he wasn't. He was definitely the muscle of the operation. It all seemed so cliché. I wondered if he had a pinky ring, like in the movies. I peeked my head around the seat and saw a gold ring on his little finger curled around the steering wheel.

I stifled a laugh and Jared's eyes shot to the rearview mirror.

"Is something funny?" he snarled.

"No, no," I said, holding my hands up innocently. It probably wasn't a good idea to tell him my thoughts and comparing him to the typical villain on television.

"There's nothing funny about the situation you're in, sweetheart. Your sister crossed the wrong people. It's too bad you're the one who has to pay. Well, not just you, but your sugar daddy." Lenin laughed to himself.

My heart dropped. I wondered what Justin was doing or thinking right now. I was still fuming that they had taken my phone to call him in the middle of the night. I had tried to fight Jared off when he grabbed my purse, but he was too strong. My arms were still sore from where his fingers had dug into me.

After everything I had done to protect Justin and keep him out of this mess, it was all for nothing. I was being used as a pawn to get to him. When Lenin called him, I had prayed he wouldn't answer. I wanted him to be so mad at me that he wouldn't answer, or I wanted him to be asleep. Unfortunately, he picked up. *Damn you, Justin*, I thought. I had tried to warn him by yelling out, but Jared had quickly covered my mouth, stifling my cry for help.

I had strained my ears to listen to what Justin was saying on the other line, but could only hear Lenin and his demands. Justin must have agreed because Lenin gave him a time and location to meet. A strip mall at 10 a.m. Had he really agreed to pay this man thirty thousand dollars?

I hoped he would change his mind and not come. I didn't deserve his help. Not after everything I had said to him. I had broken his heart. I had used his weaknesses against him.

Now, I glanced at the clock on the dash. It was 9:30. It was almost time. I felt another wave of nausea roll over me. I clutched my stomach and tried to suck in some deep breaths.

The car slowly pulled into the parking lot of the strip mall. I had never been here before. It looked abandoned. All the storefronts were missing signs and the windows were boarded up. I realized there was no one here to help me. I sunk back into my seat, feeling defeated.

Jared winded the car through the parking lot and parked it in the back, near some overflowing dumpsters. He and Lenin got out of the car and stretched. They talked for a few minutes. I couldn't make out what they were saying.

Then I realized, maybe this was my chance to escape. They were distracted. I kept my eye on them and reached my hand over to the door. My fingers wrapped around the door handle and pulled. Nothing happened. I tried again, watching them cautiously. I pressed the unlock button and tried the door again. Nothing. It was child locked. Damn that setting.

Jared suddenly looked at me and came around to open my door. He waited for me to get out, but I stayed in my seat.

"You either get out, or I make you get out." He glared at me impatiently.

I rolled my eyes as I slid across the seat and climbed out of the car.

"Thatta girl. Do what you're told. I'm sure pretty boy likes that about you."

I shot him a look and watched as he leaned in closer. His hot breath was against my ear and I shuddered.

"I'm sure he likes a lot of things about you," he whispered as his fingers traced down my back. I closed my eyes, just hoping it would stop.

"That's enough, Jared," said Lenin pointedly before striding toward a back entrance door.

Jared removed his hand from my back and stepped away from me.

"Looks like you always do what you're told, too. Go on, follow your master." I smirked at him.

"Move." He pointed after Lenin.

I didn't budge. I was not someone to be told what to do. Ever. I could feel anger bubbling up inside of me.

"No, but really. Did you base your entire personality off shitty seventies TV shows?" I asked him. As soon as the words left my mouth, I knew I shouldn't have said it.

The back of his hand met my face in one swift movement. My eyes stung with tears, but I didn't react. I fought back my tears. I would not let him see my cry. I would remain emotionless.

"I would shut your mouth if I were you," he snapped.

It took everything in me not to kick him in the balls.

He shoved me forward. I slowly followed Lenin, who was waiting for us. He tapped his foot impatiently as he held the door open. Jared gave me another shove into the building. I stumbled forward. My eyes struggled to adjust to the dimly lit hallway. The strip lights flickered above, threatening to go off at any moment.

We walked down the hallway until we came to another door. Lenin unlocked it and ushered me inside. The room was about as big as the loft above the bar. It had a desk and a dingy couch pushed up against the wall. There was a closet door in the corner of the room. There were multiple surveillance TVs of the parking lot and surrounding the building. I scanned them quickly, hoping not to see Justin on the screen.

"Sit," demanded Lenin, pointing to the couch.

I heard Jared take a step toward me, to no doubt shove me again. I didn't give him the satisfaction. I walked to the couch and sat down.

"Good girl." Lenin sat at the desk, facing me. He brought his fingertips together and looked toward the surveillance TVs.

"Now we wait for pretty boy to show up."

"There has to be another way. Please," I pleaded.

"No offense, but you don't have what I need."

"You can have the bar," I said quickly. The last thing I wanted was to give this awful man the keys to my father's legacy, but I was desperate. I wanted to keep Justin out of this, and if it meant losing the thing I loved, then so be it.

Lenin laughed. "What am I going to do with a shitty bar?"

I pressed my lips together. It didn't work. He didn't want the bar.

"There has to be something we can work out."

"Sorry, sweetheart. The only thing I want is money and your boyfriend has a lot of it. I looked into him. Some financial whiz. Rich daddy.

His life is made. You picked a good one." He winked.

I sat back against the couch, stewing in anger. I didn't know what else I could do. I had nothing to offer this man. His mind was set, and it was set on Justin. I watched the screens waiting for a sign of life outside, but saw nothing.

Oh, God. Lenin had told him about the baby. I put my head in my hands and closed my eyes. This was not how I wanted Justin to find out. Now that he knew, there was no question he would come. All this time I had been so worried he would get scared or run, but sitting here with my life on the line, the truth became so clear.

He was everything I knew him to be, even though I had tried to convince myself otherwise. He was going to come rescue me. He was going to come slay the dragon. At least, I hoped.

Chapter 28

Justin

I pulled into the strip mall parking lot and drove around, looking for any signs of life. The place was a ghost town. It must have closed down years ago, and was probably awaiting demolition to build something new. Unfortunately, that meant I was on my own out here, at least until Kenny arrived.

I rounded the outskirts of the strip mall and spotted a black town car parked near the back of the building. That had to be Lenin's. Bridget had to be here somewhere. In what condition, I did not know. I couldn't think about it without feeling sick.

As Kenny had instructed, I drove my car to the east side of the parking lot. I eased into a parking spot and checked the time on the dash: 9:50. It was almost go-time. I glanced at the briefcase next to me in the passenger seat. It was stacked full of hundreds. Thirty thousand to be exact.

Just then, Kenny's sports car pulled up next to me. A large, blacked-out SUV pulled up next to his. I watched as Kenny got out of his car, followed by two of the biggest guys from the team who got out of the SUV. They walked toward me as I pushed my car door open. I clambered out and looked at Kenny thankfully.

"Hey, man. Thanks for coming," I said.

He pulled me in for a hug and a few pats on the back.

"Of course. I've always got your back, and Bridget's. You know Chad and Sterling."

I nodded at them. "Hey. Thanks, guys, for doing this," I said genuinely. I meant it. I felt an overwhelming amount of thanks for these guys who hardly knew me to risk their wellbeing. I knew they weren't here for me, but more so for Bridget. She was like family to them. Murphy's was their spot. There was history there.

"Of course. If anyone messes with Bridget, or any of our Murphy's family, we'll mess them up," said Sterling, cracking his knuckles.

"Kenny didn't have to ask me twice. How did Bridget even get into this mess?" asked Chad, his eyes filled with concern. I knew he had a thing for her. It was obvious whenever I had seen him come into the bar. Kenny had told me too. It wasn't a big surprise he was here to help. I appreciated it nonetheless.

"Long story," I said.

"Did you scope the place out?" asked Kenny, peering at the abandoned building.

"Yeah, I spotted a town car just over there. It's tucked in the back." I walked to the passenger side of my car and opened the door. I grabbed the briefcase and shut the door behind me.

"Let's go then," said Kenny.

I noticed him adjust something in his back pocket as he walked ahead of me. It was a small pistol. I wondered where he had gotten it from. Kenny didn't seem like the kind of guy who would own a gun. We were dealing with a criminal, or at least a wannabe gangster, maybe it was good to have a weapon. At the very least, it could scare them.

We walked toward the building swiftly. My eyes scanned it as we approached to make sure we hadn't been spotted. I didn't see anyone, though. I could feel my nerves reaching my chest, causing my heart to race. Having Kenny and his guys here made me feel better, but I was still anxious. I didn't want anything to go wrong.

I just wanted to get Bridget out of here. I didn't care about the money, or that this guy was taking advantage of me. Yeah, it pissed me off a little, but mostly because the woman I cared for was involved. He had kidnapped her, for God's sake. I needed to see that she was okay. Even after our fight the night before, none of that mattered.

As we approached the building, we looked around to see which door we should enter. There were several back doors for the stores that used to be here.

"Now what?" asked Kenny quietly.

I shrugged. Lenin hadn't given me any more details past 10 a.m. at the strip mall. I tried opening one of the doors. It was locked. I tried another. The same thing. I wondered if I should knock. I checked the phone for the time: 9:57. We were here right on time.

After a moment, we heard a door unlock and swing open. A tall, bald man stepped outside, holding the door open with his large hand. He wore a shabby, faded suit that was ill-fitting. I sized him up quickly. He was huge, but we could take him if it came down to it.

"Which one of you is Justin?" he asked, looking at each of us.

I stepped forward.

"Where is Bridget?" I asked sternly.

"Ahh, there you are." He smirked at me.

"Where is she?" I asked again.

"She's a real firecracker, that one. I can see why you like her," he said. "Tell me, how is she in bed?"

I immediately filled with rage. I felt my face turning crimson as my breath became shortened.

"What did you say?" I asked, narrowing my gaze. I took a step forward.

"Calm down," whispered Kenny, stepping alongside me.

"We have your boss's money, asshole. Take us to Bridget," Kenny said to the man.

Chad and Sterling stepped up next to us to show that we meant business, and we had power. The man assessed us for a moment and nodded for us to follow him. We walked behind him through the door and into a dim hallway. The lights above flickered, playing tricks on my eyes. I hoped we hadn't just walked into a trap.

A few yards down the hallway, the man stopped and unlocked a door. He opened it slightly, so a small sliver of light escaped.

"Just you," he said, nodding at me. He put his arm up to stop Kenny and the other guys from following behind me.

"W-what?" I stammered.

"They stay out here."

"We'll be right here," said Kenny assuredly. In the darkness, he slipped the pistol from his pocket and pressed it into my hand. The henchman didn't notice. It felt heavy in my hand. I slid it into my back pocket, pulling my shirt over to hide it.

I pushed the door open the rest of the way and entered a small room, the door closing behind me. There in front of me was Bridget. She sat on the couch with Lenin towering over her. I sucked in a breath of relief as her eyes met mine. She was here. She was okay.

I took a giant step toward her, but Lenin quickly stepped in front of me, blocking me.

"Not so fast, Mr. Ralston," said Lenin, putting his hand up. "Did you bring what I asked?"

I shoved the briefcase into his chest, causing him to stumble slightly.

"It's all there," I said.

"You won't mind if I count it then?" he asked, steadying himself as he clutched the case of money.

"Be my guest," I said, annoyed.

He smiled. I watched with horror as Lenin grabbed a handful of Bridget's hair and pulled her up from the couch. She let out a yelp of pain.

"Get your hands off of her!" I shouted, taking a step toward him.

"Uh uh uh," he said, dropping the briefcase to the floor. He opened the flap of his suit and revealed a gun tucked in his pocket.

My stomach did a flip and I stopped in my tracks. I put my hands up as if to say I understood.

"Thatta boy," he said, eyeing me cautiously. He picked up the briefcase once more.

He pulled Bridget alongside him toward the desk. She struggled to keep up as I watched helplessly. I felt the weight of the pistol in my back pocket, but I didn't want to fight fire with fire. Someone could get hurt. Bridget could get hurt. I would have to just be patient, and keep this guy happy until he released her.

"Open it," he commanded Bridget, shoving her against the desk. She winced in pain.

As she shakily unclicked the clasps of the briefcase, I noticed the bruises on her arms. Purple marks in the shapes of fingers circled her upper arms. One cheek was red and tender. Her lower lip was crusted over in dried blood. Both eyes were swollen and red. I felt sick with rage. What had they done to her?

She slowly opened the briefcase, revealing the money inside. Lenin's eyes scanned the stacks of cash. He used one hand to sift through it. His mind was busy counting. After a minute or two, he looked up at me. He seemed satisfied. He released his grip on Bridget, who ran toward me.

She nearly knocked me down as I wrapped my arms around her, catching her. I was afraid to hold her too tightly. I didn't want to hurt her. I breathed her in, trying to convince myself this was real. She was safe. I had saved her.

Her dream had been right. As ridiculous as it all sounded when she told me about her dream and how it must mean something, it was all real. Now, I just needed to get her out of here and make sure this man would never touch her again.

"You have the money. It's all there. We'll be leaving now," I said.

"Yeah, yeah," said Lenin, waving me off as he continued stacking the money.

I took a step toward him, keeping Bridget behind me. Lenin looked up at me, annoyed.

"You'll be leaving her and me alone now. Do you understand?" I said, my eyes narrowed.

I watched him roll his eyes. He needed a little more convincing.

"I'm serious. You come near her again and you'll regret it," I said, pulling the pistol from my pocket and slamming it on the desk.

Two could play this game. I heard Bridget gasp as Lenin's eyes fell to the pistol. A look of understanding passed over them. He nodded. I placed the pistol back in my pocket.

"It's just business," said Lenin with a shrug, but I could see he now saw me as a threat. Little did he know, the real threat would be the police, who I fully intended on calling later. I couldn't trust this man to leave us alone for good. I needed to keep Bridget safe.

"Well, our business ends here, you greedy pig."

I turned and wrapped my arm around Bridget, leading her to the door. I wanted to get the hell out of here before this guy changed his mind. She held onto me tightly as I opened the door, leading her into the dark hallway. Kenny and the guys quickly stood from leaning against the wall, looks of relief washing over them when they spotted Bridget. She looked taken aback at the sight of them.

"Oh, thank God," said Kenny with a sigh of relief.

"Well, it's been a pleasure, boys. Miss Quinn," said Lenin's henchman.

I stepped in front of her. I didn't want his eyes to be so lucky as to look at her again. He gave a little laugh as he entered the room to join Lenin, closing the door behind him. I followed Kenny and the guys down the hallway, and out the door to the parking lot.

The sun felt warm on my face as I held Bridget tightly against me. I led her toward the car, the guys trailing behind us to make sure no one was following us. She didn't say anything. She just walked in silence, clutching tightly to me. I knew in that moment that I would never let her go again.

Chapter 29

Bridget

I clutched Justin tightly, my fingers pulling at his shirt as I tried to get closer. I couldn't believe he was here. This was real. He had come to save me. I lay my head against his shoulder as we walked. I listened to his breath slow and breathed in his familiar scent. His fingers grazed gently up and down my arm.

I could hear Kenny, Chad, and Sterling walking behind us murmuring among themselves. I couldn't believe they were here too. I was shocked when I saw them waiting in the hallway. Never would I have believed that anyone would come together to help me in this way.

Justin must have called them, and I was glad he did. Lenin and Jared were dangerous. If anything were to have gone wrong, I was glad Justin had backup. I would never forgive myself if something bad had happened to him, or them.

Despite my initial hopes he wouldn't come because of the danger I had put him in, I was hit with a wave of relief when he walked in that room. It felt like the air had been knocked out of me just at the sight of him. I knew in that moment that I needed him in my life. Not to save me, but to be with me. I had fallen for him. It only took a shady loan shark kidnapping me to realize it.

We reached Justin's car at the far end of the parking lot. He slipped his hand through mine as he thanked the guys for helping out. They patted Justin on the back. I wanted to thank them, but the words failed to come. I just looked at them, fighting back tears. They nodded as if they understood.

"We're just glad you're safe, Bridg," said Kenny softly.

"I won't be needing this," said Justin, as he reached into his pocket and handed Kenny the pistol. I had been shocked to see him pull it on Lenin earlier. It had delivered the message though, and no one got hurt.

Kenny tucked it in his back pocket, and turned to get in his car. Chad and Sterling gave me small, reassuring smiles as they loaded up into their SUV. Justin and I watched as they drove away, and that was when it all hits me. The weight of everything seemed to crash onto my shoulders, causing my knees to buckle. I fell slightly, but Justin caught me and pulled me in close. Quiet sobs escaped me as I collapsed into his arms.

"It's okay, baby. You're safe now," he whispered before he kissed the top of my head.

It felt surreal to be here standing in the sunshine with this incredible man when not even eight hours ago, I was being abducted. I had tried to be strong, but I didn't know if I would make it out of that storm. I only hoped it was really over.

"I can't believe you came," I whispered.

"Of course I did," he said, pulling away to look at me. His eyes were deep green and filled with worry. I had done that to him. I felt terrible. I reached my hand up and pressed my palm gently against his cheek.

He smiled softly down at me. "Let me take you home," he said.

"I don't want to go home. I don't feel safe there. Can I go home with you?"

I realized I had never been to his place, but it was probably safer than my brownstone.

"Of course." He nodded.

Justin pulled his keys from his pocket and unlocked the car doors, then opened the passenger door and helped me inside. He put my seatbelt on and looked me over before gently closing the door. He jogged to the driver's side and slid inside.

"Let's get the hell out of here," he said, reaching for my hand and giving it a gentle squeeze.

We drove in silence away from that awful place and into the familiar city. He never let go of my hand. My fingers lay intertwined with his on his lap. I was thankful for that because his touch made me feel safe. Made him feel real. I had never been one to be clingy, but I didn't know if I'd ever be able to let him go after that nightmare.

As I looked out the window, his thumb stroking my hand, I thought about how it could have been so much worse. Yes, I would probably have nightmares about it for a while. I would probably be paranoid that I was being watched. I would probably not want to be alone for a long, long time. I had been roughed up a little, but I had gotten out. Thanks to Justin, who sat here beside me. The man who had paid my ransom and come to rescue me.

One of the things that hurt the most was that it was all because of my sister. Someone who was supposed to love me and have my back. She was my family, and she had put me in danger knowingly. She had left *me* to pay her debt. She had left *me* to pick up her life that was in pieces. I would probably never forgive her for this. I didn't see how I could.

"We're almost there," said Justin, lifting my hand and kissing it.

He turned down a street and I saw a large, glass high-rise condominium come into view. He pulled up to the parking garage attendant and held his card up. The attendant waved him through and he wound the car expertly down two levels to his parking spot. He turned off the car and reached for the handle on the door.

I knew I had to say something. I grabbed his hand.

He stopped and turned to look at me.

"Thank you," I said softly.

"Bridget, you know I would do anything for you."

I pulled my hand away as my gaze dropped to my lap. "I don't deserve you. Not after what I said to you last night."

"Bridget…"

"No, let me finish. I said horrible, cruel things to you. I didn't mean any of it. I just got so scared. I thought if hurt you, really hurt you, you would stay away."

"Why would you want me to stay away?"

"I was scared of getting hurt. I was scared of *you* getting hurt. I'm a mess, Justin."

"You're not a mess," he said softly, lifting his hand and tucking my hair behind my ear.

"You just had to save me from a kidnapping." I laughed softly. It felt good to laugh.

He smiled at me and pressed his forehead against mine. "Worth it," he whispered.

He pulled away and looked at me.

"What?" I asked, studying his face.

"Is it true?"

"Is what true?" I asked.

"Are you pregnant?"

My stomach suddenly felt like it was swarmed by a million butterflies. I felt like I might throw up. With everything that had happened, I had forgotten that the secret was out. He knew about the baby, thanks to Lenin.

"I am…" I said hesitantly.

"Bridget! This is amazing." He grabbed my face and kissed my forehead several times.

"What? Really?" I asked, shocked.

"Of course. I'm going to be a dad!"

Excitement was dancing in his eyes, and for the first time, I felt excited. I had been so scared to tell him that there was no room for any other emotion, but now my eyes filled with tears of happiness.

"I was so scared to tell you," I said, biting my lip.

"I understand, but you didn't need to be. Bridget, I'm going to be there for you and this baby. Our baby. If you'll let me."

I nodded as the tears fell down my cheeks. We held each other for several minutes.

"Let's get you inside," he said, pulling away. I noticed him wipe a tear from his cheek, and my heart filled.

He opened the car door and came around to open mine, then held out his hands and gently pulled me out of the car. He slipped his arm around my waist as he led me to the elevator and slid his keycard through the reader. The elevators opened up and a doorman stood inside, giving us a warm smile.

"Mr. Ralston." He nodded as he pressed the button to the top floor.

This place was like a fortress. I felt safer already. The elevator doors opened to a condo that was bigger than my brownstone and

Murphy's combined. I sucked in a breath as I looked around the large entryway.

Justin reached for my hand and led me down one of the large hallways. I tried to keep up as I took in my surroundings. I could get lost in here. He led me through two large double doors, through what I assumed was his bedroom, and into a large marble bathroom.

He pulled a plush white towel from a glass shelf and placed it on the edge of the tub. He turned on the water until steam wafted up.

"Bubbles?" he asked.

"Yes, please." I smiled.

He grabbed a bottle and poured a capful of liquid soap in. The smell of lavender filled the air.

"Well, I'll leave you to it," he said, turning to leave.

I grabbed his hand and pulled him close. He looked down at me and then to my lips. My eyes fluttered closed and I waited with anticipation for what I wanted since I saw him walk through the door in that rundown building. He kissed me softly before turning and closing the door behind him.

I slipped into the delicious hot water and let out a deep breath. I leaned my head against the back of the tub and let the bubbles run over me. He was going to take care of me, and I him. Not only that, he was going to take care of our baby.

We were going to be a family. I sunk deeper into the tub as I let contentment wash over me.

After a long soak, I wrapped myself in the towel Justin had left out for me. I peeked into the bedroom, but he wasn't there. I padded down through the room and to the hallway. I heard his voice coming from the living room we had passed earlier.

"That's right, officer. The abandoned strip mall. He runs his operations out of there."

I looked around the corner and saw Justin on the phone, pacing.

"I don't care about the money. If I never get it back, it won't matter. I just want this guy off the streets," he continued.

He looked up then and saw me standing there. He smiled.

"Keep me updated, please," he said and ended the call.

He tossed his phone on the couch and walked over to me, taking me in his arms. His hands felt smooth against my damp skin. I leaned in to him and looked up at him.

"You called the cops?" I asked.

"I had to. I knew it was the only way to keep you truly safe."

I nodded and nuzzled my head into his chest. His heartbeat thudded softly. I felt relieved at the thought that Lenin would be arrested and locked up. He would never come after me or anyone again. I knew I would never be able to live a normal life knowing he was out there. I would never feel fully safe. I also felt some relief for my sister. Though I would probably never speak to her again, knowing she would be safe made me feel better.

"Thank you," I whispered.

"I'll always keep you safe, Bridget. You and our baby. I love you."

"I love you, too."

Chapter 30

Bridget

I watched from the second-story window as Justin balanced a large box in one arm while shutting the moving truck door with the other. He must have felt my eyes on him because he looked up at that moment, rain falling in his eyes. He smiled at me before readjusting the box in his arms and walking up the steps.

With my own smile, I finished unpacking the box I was working on, and carried his toiletries to the bathroom. I placed them gently on the counter, then picked up his bottle of cologne and inhaled the familiar scent before setting it back down on the counter. I ran my fingertips over the bottles and felt an overwhelming amount of happiness come over me.

I couldn't believe he was carrying boxes of his belongings into my place. It seemed surreal. Ever since he'd saved me from that asshole, Lenin, we had been inseparable. I thought back to the night he brought me home. We had stayed up all night talking about everything, which wasn't new for us, but this time we didn't talk about our favorite foods or movies. We went deeper.

"How is this going to work?" I had asked as I lay on the couch, my head nestled in his lap.

"What? Us?" he asked.

"Yeah…"

"Well, you already know I love you. And our baby." He placed his hand on my stomach gently.

"I know. I love you, too, but are you ready for all of this? It all happened so fast. I don't want you to feel like you're…trapped." My insecurities were dancing together in my head, and I knew I had to be honest. I had to know.

"I told you at the bar that night before you ripped my heart out and stomped on it—"

"Sorry about that. You know I was just trying to protect you," I interrupted softly.

He kissed me on the forehead. "I know that now. But before all that, and before I knew about the baby, I told you I wanted to be with you. Nothing could change that. You have to know that."

"I do. Now. I just wanted to lay it all out on the table."

"I love you. I want to be with you. I want to be a family. There, it's all out on the table for me. Go."

I rolled onto my back and looked up at him. He smiled down at me reassuringly.

"Ditto," I said.

We spent the next few weeks at his place, while we stayed informed by law enforcement about what was going on with Lenin. It took them some time to actually find him, despite Justin giving them a lead. While those weeks were stressful, they were also blissful.

We stayed holed up in his penthouse playing house. I got Andy to cover the bar for me. I thought it best to stay put in case Lenin came looking for me again. Andy said yes with no hesitation after I explained what had happened. I was grateful for him.

It was probably for the best because the first trimester was no joke. The morning sickness didn't live up to its name. It should be called all day and all night sickness. I was exhausted all the time. Justin took good care of me. Always running to the store for ginger ale or ice cream or pepperoncini. His shopping list was always a mix of what I was craving or what would help stop me from throwing up. I thought I would be embarrassed by him seeing me at my worst, but he didn't care. He was right there with me, holding my hair and rubbing my back.

Justin worked from home most days, with the occasional meetings elsewhere. When he wasn't working and when I wasn't in the bathroom or asleep, we would do nothing and everything. If I didn't love him enough before, I grew to love him even more. We played board games. For a financial advisor, he sure sucked at Monopoly. He took my wins like a champ, though. We cooked our way through one of his cookbooks, eating dinner out on the patio and watching the sun set. We spent a lot of time in his California king bed. It almost felt like a honeymoon.

When we got word that Lenin and Jared had been arrested, we celebrated with champagne for Justin and sparkling cider for me. I was finally feeling better now that I was in my second trimester. Now that I was safe, we had talked about what came next. With the baby's due date approaching, we had some decisions to make.

We decided to move in together, officially. I had been staying at his place for weeks, but we hadn't fully meshed our lives together yet. The stall in the arrest of Lenin had stalled our plans, but now we were free to live our normal lives again.

We talked about the pros and cons of both of our places, but Justin was the one who expressed his desire to move into my brownstone with me. I was surprised, because here, he had this huge penthouse with amazing views of the city, and he wanted to leave. But he had fallen in love with my two-story townhome when he visited for the first time.

As I looked around my place now, I did too. It was the perfect place to raise a baby. It was small, but it was warm. I could see many memories being made here. Carrying our baby up the stairs, avoiding the spots that creaked. Rocking in my rocking chair under the small, circular window, looking at the stars. First steps padding on the oak wood floors. I could see it all.

I also wanted to start working at the bar again, and decided I wanted to hire more staff. I didn't want to be working all the time with the baby's due date approaching, and especially when the baby was here. I was still the owner, and still wanted to work part-time, but I was also ready to let go of the reins a bit.

"Hey, babe," Justin called up the stairs just then.

"Yeah?" I called down.

"Cleo and Kenny are back with the final load."

"I'll be right down!"

Cleo and Kenny had offered to help us move. They had really been such great friends through everything. Kenny coming to back up Justin in a dangerous situation, and Cleo constantly checking in on me afterward with a basket of baked goods. I was lucky to have them.

I held the banister as I walked down the stairs. Cleo walked through the door, holding a box from the bakery.

"I figured you'd need snacks, prego." She held up the box.

"Oh, you figured right." I opened the lid and saw mouthwatering croissants, donuts, and scones. I grabbed a glazed donut and took a big bite.

"Perfection," I said, closing my eyes.

Cleo laughed and put her hand on my growing belly. "Baby gets only the best pastries," she said.

Kenny and Justin walked in then, carrying large boxes stacked on top of one another.

"Daaaang," cat-called Cleo.

They laughed as they brought the boxes to the living room. Justin's hair was damp with sweat or the rain. Either way, he looked good. My eyes grazed over his tense muscles as he placed the boxes on the floor. Pregnant or not, he still did something for me. Now, if we could just get our friends out of here. I loved them, I did, but I was ready for some alone time with Justin in our new home.

Justin walked over and wrapped his arms around me, placing his hands on my belly. I held up the last bit of my donut and he took the last bite before kissing me on the neck. I felt my face flush.

"Well, that looks like it's the last of it," said Cleo, looking at me knowingly.

"Are you sure? Do you guys want any more help unpacking?" asked Kenny.

"I think we've got it," said Justin.

"Thank you, guys. For everything," I said. After all, they had been the two to introduce Justin and me.

We all hugged goodbye and I walked them out, waving as they jogged to their car in the rain. I closed the door and walked back to the living room where Justin was opening boxes. I grabbed his hand and tugged him to follow me. I led him up the stairs and to my—our—bedroom. The rain was pitter-pattering against the roof and the streetlights had just come on, casting a warm glow through the window.

"Welcome home," I whispered as I wrapped my hands around the back of his neck.

His lips curled into a smile, as his hands trailed down the back of my arms and down my sides, barely touching me, but leaving a burning impression all the same. I tilted my chin up, inviting his lips to touch mine. Instead, he trailed them across my jawbone and down my neck. I threw my head back, enjoying the sensation of his breath against my skin.

He guided me back toward the bed, his eyes intent on mine. When the back of my knees met the mattress, I fell back onto the plush duvet. I looked up at Justin expectantly as he stood over me, his damp T-shirt clinging to the curve of his muscles. God, he was so sexy.

I parted my legs slowly, letting the hem of my dress ride up and reveal my lace panties. I watched as his eyes slowly traveled down.

"You mean to tell me you had these on all day?" he asked as he took a step toward me, placing a knee on the bed.

I nodded. He knelt over me as his hungry eyes took me in.

"We should have kicked Kenny and Cleo out a long time ago," he said.

I laughed.

Justin's hands moved slowly up my inner thighs until they met the waistband of my panties. His fingers hooked underneath and slid them off me with ease. His hands were back on me, lifting my hips and pulling me closer to the edge of the bed. He slid to the floor and knelt in front of me, his fingers gripped around my hips as he brought his mouth to me. At the feeling of his tongue lapping against me, I fell back into the bed weakly. I lost all control when it came to him.

As he began kissing me deeper, I grabbed his hair in my hands, pulling desperately. My back hitched, but he held me firmly against the bed. As every sensation in my body came to an electrifying head, I grabbed the blankets tightly as I exploded.

I lay there breathless, looking at the ceiling, until I propped myself on my elbows and looked down at him. He licked his lips as he smiled up at me. I sat up and tugged on his shirt, and he smiled and peeled it over his head, revealing his toned body. I leaned forward and kissed his chest before trailing my tongue against his neck. My hands slid down his body until they met the waistband of his sweats. I pulled them down, revealing his large erection just inches from me.

I spread my legs, inviting him in. He looked down with a sly smile before guiding the tip of himself into me slowly, inch by inch. His hand grabbed my lower back, pulling me closer, filling me completely. I moved against him, grinding, until he couldn't possibly be deeper. He brought his mouth to mine. We stayed intertwined for a moment, our breaths heavy and in sync. It was our first time making love in our home. We were soaking it in. And then he moved out of me, before crashing back into me again, bringing me to the brink again.

Afterwards, we lay in bed completely spent from the move and from making love. I lay breathlessly on my back with Justin's arm cradled around the crook of my neck. He turned his head toward me and his eyes wandered to my growing belly. He gently placed his hand on me.

"It's probably time you start taking it easy for baby. All the heavy lifting and all of *that* is probably too much for the little guy. Or girl."

"I won't be stopping *that* any time soon, but I'll gladly let you take over the moving boxes."

Justin laughed. "You've got it."

"What do you think baby is?" I asked, placing my hand over his.

"I'll be happy with either one. Even happier if he or she has your red hair."

Just then, I felt the baby kick for the first time. I looked at Justin to see if he felt it too. His eyes teared up as we lay there, hopeful for the future.

Epilogue

Justin

I straightened my tie in the bathroom mirror, stealing a glance at Bridget, who was touching up her lipstick. I noticed her hand was shaking.

I rested my hand on her arm and gave her a gentle squeeze. "It's all going to be over today," I said softly.

She let out the breath she had been holding and looked at me in the mirror. "Thanks, babe."

I checked my watch. It was 8:30 a.m. We had to be at the courthouse in thirty minutes.

"We should probably go," I said.

She nodded knowingly, and put the cap on the tube of lipstick. I pulled her into my arms and gave her a kiss on the forehead. Today was a big day. We were going to trial and hopefully sending Lenin away for good. Although he had been locked up all this time, I knew Bridget's fears wouldn't be put to rest until he was convicted.

I followed behind her as we made our way downstairs. I had never seen her in a suit before. The cream skirt and blazer looked good on her.

Too good. I would happily take it off later. For now, I gave her a little pat on the behind.

She whipped around and raised her eyebrows playfully.

"What?" I shrugged. "I feel like we're role playing or something."

She let out a laugh. A real one. I was happy to make her smile when her nerves were shot.

"That's for later." She grabbed my tie and pulled me in for a kiss. "But now, we have to go make sure this asshole gets what he deserves."

When we arrived at the courthouse, I saw Kenny and Cleo waiting outside. They were here for moral support, and Kenny was also a witness. We all walked in together, collectively holding our breaths.

Hours later, we walked outside with smiles on our faces. Bridget let out a relieved sigh as she laid her head on my chest. I wrapped my arms around her and hugged her tight.

"We did it," she whispered.

And we had. Lenin was sentenced to twenty years in prison for kidnapping, issuing illegal loans, and organized crime. The police had found more evidence of his illegal doings in the secret office at the strip mall. Jared was tried at a lesser sentence as an accomplice.

"*You* did, babe. You were amazing up there," I said, kissing the top of her head.

"We should celebrate!" said Kenny triumphantly.

"Definitely!" agreed Cleo.

Half an hour later, we were at Murphy's. Andy opened the bar early and all the regulars were walking through the door to celebrate their favorite bar owner's victory. Kenny had called the guys from the team, including the team's owner, Jonas, and his wife, Mae. It was turning into a real party.

I lifted Bridget up onto the bar top and she laughed joyfully.

"To Bridget!" I shouted, holding up a pint of beer.

"To Bridget!" Kenny shouted in agreement, clinking his glass to mine.

Bridget held up her glass of water and rubbed her very round belly. She looked beautiful as she gazed down at everyone excitedly. I couldn't be any more in love with this woman. We were finally able to move on with our lives—and just in time, too, because our baby boy would be here soon.

This is the end of Brigdet and Justin's love story.

Want to be notified when the next book in the series is released?

Or would you like to read a free romance novel from me instead?

For both - subscribe:
https://BookHip.com/LHLBBPG

Printed in Great Britain
by Amazon